Pen Pictures

Interpreting the Secrets of Handwriting

Alternatives
Life Options for Today

Pen Pictures

Interpreting the Secrets of Handwriting

PETER WEST

First published in Great Britain in 1999 by
LONDON HOUSE
114 New Cavendish Street
London W1M 7FD

A catalogue record for this book is available
from the British Library

ISBN 1 902809 05 X

Edited and designed by DAG Publications Ltd, London.
Printed and bound by Biddles Limited,
Guildford, Surrey.

Note to the Reader
Unless otherwise stated, references and interpretations
may be read for both sexes. Comments made on any of
the handwriting samples and signatures in this book are
to help highlight the basic graphological principles of that
particular example. They should not be read as a
comment on the character or personality of the writer
concerned.

Contents

Introduction

Handwriting probably began as crude drawings on cave walls, when man wanted to record his activities by showing just how brave he was to go out hunting and providing for those who depended on him. He drew images of animals, himself and his family, the sun, moon and stars, the weapons he used, friends, enemies and gods. All this occurred well over 20,000 years ago, and these drawings were the first real examples of how the hand can show what the mind and body experienced as the days progressed.

When these early archivists first met other tribes, it is highly probable they would have had to communicate in different tongues. And when these meetings first took place, they would have shown these pictures to their visitors. If the meetings were for pleasure, they might have used the wall markings to show friends how good it would be to remain that way because they, the artists, were powerful people. And of course, all this would also have been conveyed with that one universal language we all learn very early in our lives – gesture. If the visitors were enemies, or potential enemies, the emphasis might have been on showing how unwise it would be to make war. Any gestures then used would have been unmistakable!

So even in those very early days these simple etchings had their own meanings and had to be interpreted in different ways by whoever read them and for whatever purpose. Essentially, these early scribbles and their inherent meanings have not changed a great deal, right through to present times. Today gesture is still employed to convey meaning and expression that, in many cases, says much more than writing or speech ever could.

Early Trade
Trade could have been a very good reason for the first meetings and, as such gatherings became regular, the traders would have found it

necessary to mark their wares in some way to help define ownership. Seals were used as early labels, perhaps of clay, or even wood dyed in colours, and symbols of some kind inscribed on the seals soon began to be seen.

The Alphabet

Sooner or later, this rather basic identification developed into early writing in Sumeria, which is roughly equivalent to present-day Iraq. Sumer is now generally thought of as the birthplace of modern civilization. Since then there have been so many changes, additions and deletions that we would scarcely recognize these very early markings as the basis of our modern English language alphabet of 26 letters.

Writing Systems

Modern handwriting bears little relation to those early scripts. Where we normally begin writing near the top left-hand side of a sheet of paper and write in a straight line across the page, early handwriting might have been made in several ways.

One style was to alternate the direction of the script from line to line, called *boustrophedon*, or 'ox-turning'. It was of Greek origin, following the way a field is ploughed. By the fifth century BC this system had been abandoned, although the *stoichedon* system was briefly used where the writers aligned letters vertically and horizontally and also from left to right. These variations are mentioned only in passing, for this book is concerned with handwriting and the way it may be used to define character and personality, and not with the history of its development.

Identification

We learn basic handwriting skills in early childhood, and as our talents develop so does the way we write, which in turn can reflect these inclinations. As we grow older we speed up. We add little bits here and take off other little bits there. This tends to occur over a long period of time but so does the way we progress in other ways. Sooner or later, we all begin to use a style that our friends identify with us. As they get to recognize us through our handwriting so we begin to associate friends and eventually, other people, with their scripts. It is quite possible to recognize someone by their hand-writing. Think for a moment what you do when a letter arrives through the post. You probably look at it to see if you can recognize the handwriting. If you recognize the handwriting of a friend or relative you can say so quite confidently. You *know* it is from them. If you cannot identify the sender, you will turn the envelope all ways to see where it has come from, when easily the most sensible thing to do is open it. Many people do this, even today.

Curiously, at this stage in our lives we begin to become amateur graphologists ourselves, because when we become familiar with a friend's handwriting we also begin to recognize some of their personality traits. At about the same time, although we may not realize it, we begin to register that similar personality types tend to write in a similar fashion. This very early introduction to graphology is something we all experience, but few of us realize what value it could have, then or later.

Definition of Graphology
Graphology is the study and analysis of handwriting in order to interpret the character and personality of the writer. With the advice and guidance of a good analyst it can be used to show a writer where his true talents may lie, as opposed to his current occupation. People can often show aptitude in a particular field but fail to pursue it because they do not receive any support and encouragement from those around them. If a graphological assessment is made at the right time, in children, for instance, when they are beginning to show some basic inclination towards various interests, it can help plan their future life.

You cannot use graphology to detect the age or sex of a writer, but it can indicate a left- or right-handed person. It is now more or less accepted that men can show certain feminine characteristics, while women may have some masculine traits in their script. Some quite elderly people can and do write with such a firm hand you would be forgiven for thinking they were years younger. Conversely, certain illnesses in a much younger person can be mistaken for signs of great age. As a rule, the mental or intellectual maturity of a writer will be present, as well as signs of their emotional development.

The Origins of Graphology

Graphology is a relatively modern art-science, although there is an oft-quoted remark that Suetonius Tranquillus once complained of the terrible writing of Octavius Augustus, circa AD 120 in his book *De Vita Caesarum* – The Lives of the Caesars. While he may not have been criticizing as a graphologist, he was certainly complaining about the handwriting itself. The writer had obviously not planned the writing properly, but in those days it was probably written by a scribe and so he, not Caesar, was really to blame.

What the story does show is that consciousness of handwriting and writers was apparent nearly 2,000 years ago. Although writing and writing styles were evident in China in the fourth century AD, it was not until the early seventeenth century that any interest was shown in the subject in Europe. A small dissertation appeared in 1622 by Camillo Baldi, of the University of Bologna, who is credited as the founding father of modern handwriting analysis. He claimed that writing was a personal matter and did reflect character to an extent. Nearly two hundred years later, Professor Grohmann of Wittenberg made his observations known in his publication in 1792.

After this a number of prominent people began to record their acknowledgment of this kind of character analysis. The celebrated artist, Thomas Gainsborough, kept letters written by his current model pinned to his easel while he painted them. Sir Walter Scott, in his book *Chronicles of the Canongate*, makes much of early graphology when he discusses handwriting analysis. Then in 1871 a Frenchman, the Abbé Michon, coined and introduced the term graphology and was the first to create the scientific background of its study. He formulated the basic ground rules – many of which are still in use today.

Art or Science

Graphology is neither art nor science, it is both. Today, the analyst uses a scientific approach in his evaluation of all the factors in the sample of handwriting under review. The real art lies in bringing together all the traits to synthesize what he finds into a readable and acceptable word portrait. Most of this, of course, will be founded equally on the analyst's experience of life and graphology. While it is accepted that many graphologists employ some natural intuition, it is also helpful to have some element of pyschological knowledge or interest. Unless you have a basic liking or interest in what makes people tick, then you will be unable to do justice to them or yourself. Graphology, therefore, is an art-science.

Like any other discipline, the more you practise, the more you gain an insight into the behaviour patterns of people, and as you develop your interpretive skills the more it will help you understand yourself.

Rules of Interpretation

There is one very important fundamental of graphological analysis to remember at all times. The sample of handwriting you have in front of you will reflect the mood and thinking of the writer *at the time of writing*.

There are really very few exceptions to this rule. In any example of writing there are nearly always variations of letters and the overall style because the whole sample reflects the mood of the writer when the script was made. When you write a short informal note at home asking someone to do something, you write in the same basic way as you would when applying for a new job – but you would pay far more attention to the latter.

Whatever the subject, we are all self-conscious when we begin a letter but most of us generally tend to lose interest before we have gone very far. In many cases, one of the first things a graphologist would do is to turn the sample upside down and look at the end first, for it is here, at the end of a letter, that our most natural writing is found. Also, the way text is set out on the page reveals a writer's emotional, mental and physical outlook at the time of writing. Remember, it reflects the real 'inner' you.

Signatures show how writers want to be recognized by others – the 'outer' image. It is worth noting here that many people can have two signatures, often quite different. One may be used for formal, business matters and is also likely to reflect his – or the writer's – business or company status. The other signature will be used for personal, private and more intimate matters, and often reflects this personal image. This is just one of many reasons why it is unwise to analyse any one signature on its own. It may not always be possible, but there should be two, three or even four samples, all written at different times, for the analyst to consider. Ideally, it is preferable to have other samples of writing, also written at different times, for you to compare.

Envelopes, Numbers and Colours

Keep handwritten envelopes. While it is felt that an element of control is present when an envelope is addressed, it is always worthwhile making an assessment and comparison of the writing on the envelope with that of the letter inside.

Take time to look at how a writer makes his or her numbers and writes the date. This can often show the age of the writer or when they were educated. Note how figures are used when sums of money are written. Observe how the monetary symbol is written – £ for the pound, $ for the dollar etc. Most writers use a variation of blue ink, but when other colours are used, it will help to refine your assessment of the writer's inner, or real emotional character. But do make sure this is the colour the writer regularly uses, and that it was not just a note dashed off with whatever was available at the time.

The same goes for the colour of the paper used. Most people tend to use white, or a variation from pure white to cream. There are a few people, however, who have a preference for coloured paper, or even paper that may have differing shades of the same colour. Some people even use multi-coloured paper.

Basic Style

Style falls into two basic patterns which may be further divided into four main categories. The two main patterns are straight or curved handwriting. Straight writing is created with up and down movements, and if it is continuous is called angular handwriting. Another version of this may be seen in a thready style, but this may also be seen in curved or round writing. Curved writing is round and may be in either a garland fashion or arcade in appearance. In their pure state, these styles are easily recognized but can often be mistaken one for the other.

Angular handwriting shows an inflexible and decisive character.
Thread writing implies a more versatile and creative approach to life.

Garland handwriting suggests a submissive nature, friendly and adaptable.

Arcade script indicates a calculating type, formal, reserved and inclined to be secretive.

Before you continue further, now is the time to write a note in your normal handwriting to someone you know well, or to yourself, to read at a later date. Use a sheet of plain, unlined A4 white paper and try to use a fountain or ballpoint pen, not a pencil or fibre-tip. Subject matter is fairly irrelevant, but try hard to write in your usual style, or about something you may have recently experienced. Write about one hundred words or so, sign it with your usual signature, date it, properly address an envelope for the letter, then put it away and keep it safe until after you have read this book. Only then will you be able to make a considered judgment of your own handwriting.

1

Handwriting Style

The appearance of any style of writing always reflects the state of the character and personality *at the time of writing*. Handwriting is governed by the state of the nervous system and the general emotional well-being of the writer. From this, we can assess the energy, temperament and intellectual perception that was available to the writer at that time.

If a writer is emotionally upset for whatever reason the general standard of the script will show this by the amount of pressure, speed and general connections of the individual letters to each other. The spacing and connections between the words and lines will also reflect this state. When a writer experiences a shock to his mental or emotional processes, or his perception rate has been seriously affected, the basic pattern of the writing may be similarly disturbed. Conversely, when a writer enjoys a glowing feeling of euphoria then the handwriting will show this mood as well. All handwriting is conditioned by the writer's normal, overall general disposition at the time of writing.

fig 1

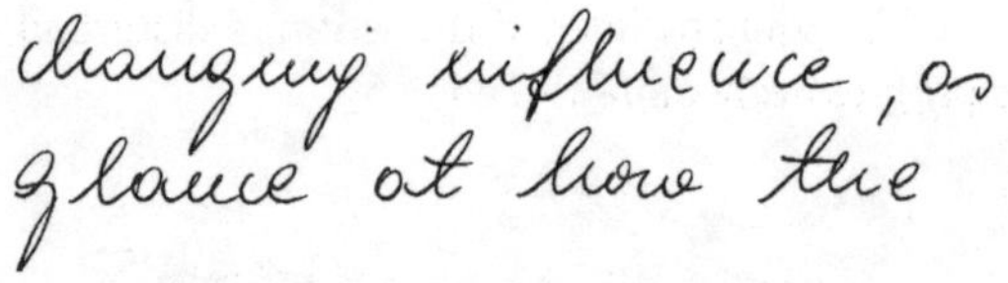

changing influence, as glance at how the

A normally warm, affectionate and receptive type will write a fluid, flowing garland script (see fig. 1). But if upset or off-balance for any reason, the handwriting will become uneven and, subject to the level of this annoyance, pressure and speed will become more evident and some angularity may creep in.

The writer who is rather reserved, difficult to get to know and inclined to be slightly calculating writes in an arcade fashion (see fig. 2). The script looks rather like a sequence of upright arches. When this writer is upset he will accentuate this arching and the pressure will be much more in evidence.

fig 2

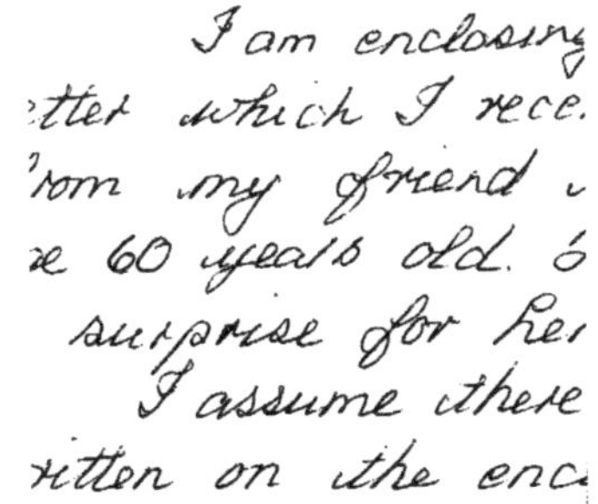

*I am enclosing
tter which I rece.
'rom my friend .
e 60 years old. ó
surprise for her
I assume there
ritten on the enc.*

A generally decisive character who rarely seems to exhibit his real, inner feelings in day-to-day dealings with others tends to write in an angular style (see fig. 3). The writing lacks the fluid curve of a garland writer and is composed more of short straight lines and connections. When this writer is disturbed the angularity will

fig 3

*The graphologist cannot
and does not need extra
or an over-developed intuition*

be much more in evidence. This writer feels he has to be all things to all men. A creative and versatile, but manipulative, oppportunistic and independent type tends to use the thready style (see fig. 4). As a rule, the script will have an easily deciphered letter here and there, but it is all connected by squiggly lines. If the writer is disturbed, this writing becomes progressively more thready.

fig 4

*handwriting to interpret
character and personality.
The graphologist cannot predict*

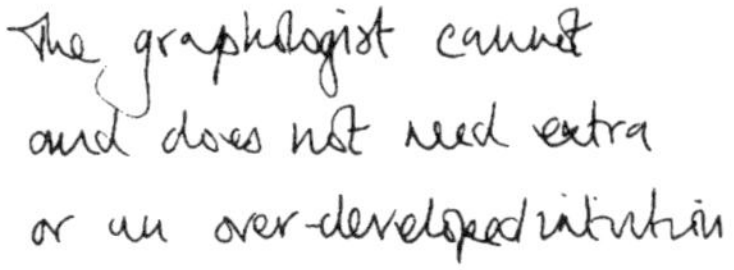

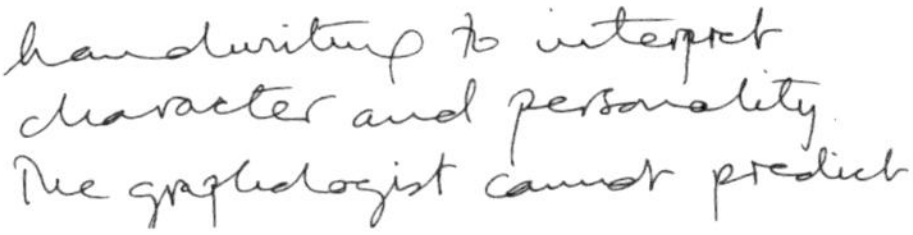

These basic personality types demonstrate the four different but clearly individualistic approaches to life with their handwriting. A normal person goes about his daily life in a recognized manner. But when thrown off-balance by an emotional or mental upset each of these types will demonstrate responses that can be easily identified by writing. Of course, there are variations on these four fundamental types which will be demonstrated as we progress through other features of handwriting analysis.

Garland handwriting

Garland writing is a relatively relaxed script. Easy to perform, it flows nicely and easily across the page, usually in a series of shallow or deep garlands not unlike the waves on a sea-shore. The writing itself indicates how open the writer is, almost as if each garland was an open bowl into which the various experiences of life may drop. The writer is ready to believe all that is said and told.

He is open, a willing participant in life's daily grind who is mostly a follower rather than a leader. He may wish to lead but he lacks the motivation, the ability to take charge. Always ready to find and believe the best of anybody, those who write in this manner are adaptable and basically non-aggressive. They respond to almost any emotional appeal, but dislike any kind of friction in their lives. They prefer to take the line of least resistance and as a rule are gentle, submissive, sympathetic and trusting. As employees they lack drive and push and tend to compromise by taking the easy way out. They are passive and non-competitive. While largely adaptable, they much prefer to deal with what they can see and understand. There is always a strong need for security. They avoid what they cannot understand and tend to clam up if or when they feel threatened in any way.

Arcade handwriting

There is a lack of ease in arcade handwriting. It looks like a series of arches which suggests a very strong self-defensive and self-protective streak in the overall make-up. The arch serves as a symbol of preservation. Indeed, this writer is so conventional he will go to a lot of trouble to preserve tradition and the proper way of doing things.

Arcade writing indicates inner independence with a strong sense of structure, caution – even secrecy. Alert and always watchful, arcade writers are often mistrustful and are quite likely to test their friendships before full acceptance. They almost always display an air of formality in their attitude.

It is difficult for them to exhibit spontaneity at any level of any relationship – in their business, romantic or social worlds. Sometimes this degree of inhibition prevents good relationships from getting off the ground. These writers can be very suspicious of people's motives, yet all this wariness can be thrown out of the window when they are called upon to display their creative and artistic talents. They become different people and, as many of them are musically inclined, they easily slip into their own magical world full of creative expression. It is here, more than anywhere, these people fully demonstrate their instinctive and intuitive understanding of the drama and theatre of self-expression.

When the arcades are shallow the writer will scheme and pretend in order to deceive. They have good memories and never forget a slight. Once they have made up their minds they stay with their decision.

Angular handwriting
Angular handwriting reveals a disciplined attitude because of the way the strokes are made. It is a controlled movement, there is no gentle curve – the pen moves abruptly up and down, often with heavy pressure. It is a slower stroke to make, suggesting a firm attitude.

These writers find it hard to adapt and have great difficulty in personal relationships. It is hard for them to compromise for they believe that firmness is all and they are very persistent types. There is a rigid, controlled personality with an inner defensive but strong-minded approach. These writers are often unyielding and determined, with fixed ideas and opinions.

If the writing is angular and extremely regular it shows a stern nature with a strong sense of obligation, without tolerance or a sense of humour. Always reliable, angular writers are aggressive and suspicious. For most, their way is the best and they try hard to impose themselves and their ideas on others. If the script is angular but irregular, the writer will have a misguided sense of resolution. He is stubborn, perhaps stemming from some inner conflict.

Angular writing rarely has loops in it, and loops are always a sign of emotion. Thus, it is easy for this type to be efficient and not worry about who they upset as they go on their way. Their emotions, if any, are kept under a very strict control.

Thread handwriting

Those who write like this are adaptable and manipulative. As a rule, thready writers are very quick-thinking individuals with a considerable talent for self-preservation and an eye on the main chance. These people turn on the charm with skill when dealing with their fellow men. While thread writing has a lack of clarity in its construction, so does the writer. He is adaptable but there is little or no clear course of action. However, these people often have a multiplicity of talents, especially in their chosen creative or artistic fields.

They see everything; they get their impressions from everyone and everywhere with their inbuilt intuition and perception. This writing marks the individualist and rebel alike, because they so often follow their own path with a total disregard for established ways of behaviour and convention.

They have an easy knack of talking themselves in and out of all difficulties, using a strategy all their own. This agility with word and deed marks their versatility and, if they really want to get to the top they will often 'arrive' early and stay there.

Thready writing with weak pressure represents a writer who will avoid his obligations. Heavy pressure suggests the free spirit, one not tied by convention but following a life of his own making. Either way, almost all thread writers will have had the benefit of a good education.

Mixed styles

Not everything comes in its purest form and unfortunately, handwriting is no exception. Often, handwriting can be a mixture of two basic styles. The dominant trend gives a clue to the way the writer will behave.

Garland and Angular

When you see garland writing with aspects of angularity in it (see fig. 5), the writer has a good sense of observation with an astute and clever mind. Strictly speaking, this is a blend of opposites. This writer will use emotional overtones to persuade others to his way of thinking but he will still not be a leader.

Further down you give examples of these you say, new York to Subtract

fig 5

Garland and Arcade

Garland and arcade writing reveals a most positive personality (see fig. 6). The writer is often creative and original, although much depends on which of the two styles dominate. This writer exercises good personal control but may be more responsive to the mood of the moment; this is a blend of two emotionally orientated styles.

fig 6

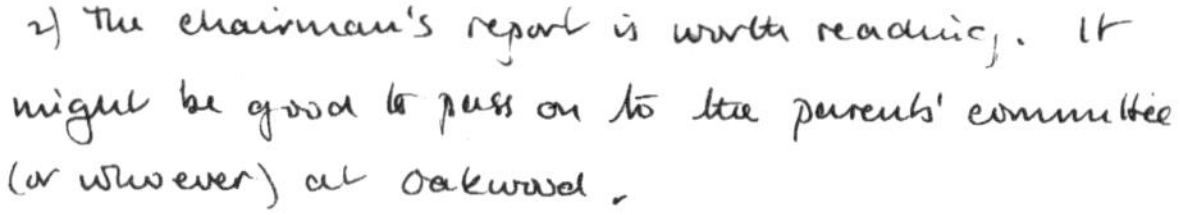

2) The chairman's report is worth reading. It might be good to pass on to the parents' committee (or whoever) at Oakwood.

Garland and Thread

This is not often seen but when it is, it is more likely to be a mix of garland with thready streaks appearing in it (see fig. 7). Generally speaking, the implication is one of poor staying power and even less concentration levels. The writer is indecisive with little resistance, but an oft-indulged lazy streak. However, once this type does begin a task it will be finished – but to the writer's satisfaction.

fig 7

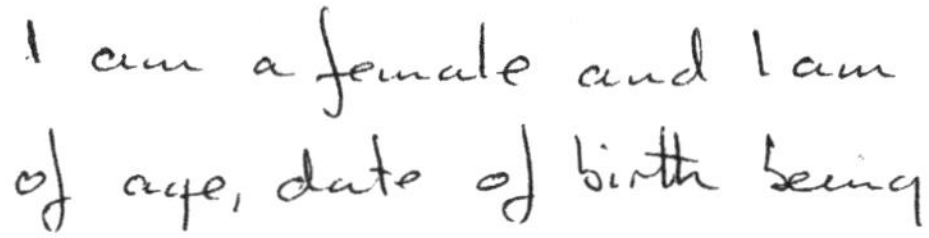

I am a female and I am of age, date of birth being

Arcade and Angular

These people are difficult to get to know and, when you do, they are equally difficult to understand. They are likely to be very critical, inflexible and intolerant. They are born perfectionists and once they get the bit between their teeth are liable to take the matter to hand to extremes. It is unwise to upset them. (Fig. 8).

fig 8

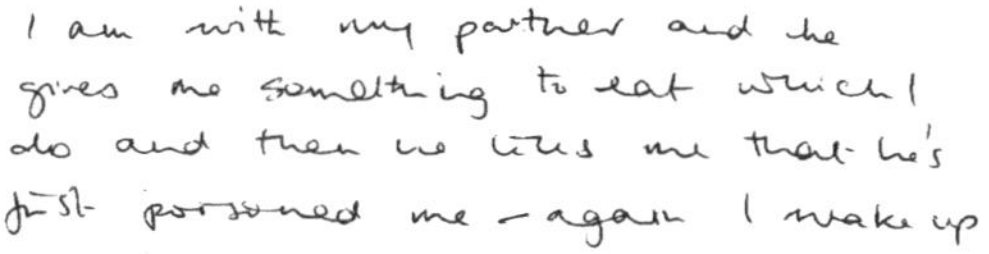

I am with my partner and he gives me something to eat which I do and then he tells me that he's just poisoned me – again I wake up

Arcade and Thread

This style of writing belongs to a persuasive and very perceptive type of personality (see fig. 9). He likes to work behind the scenes and knows how to keep a secret. There can be strong creative overtones in the overall character. The social life may be minimal for he is not overtly sociable and is disconcertingly frank or too straightforward at the best of times, which does not endear him to others.

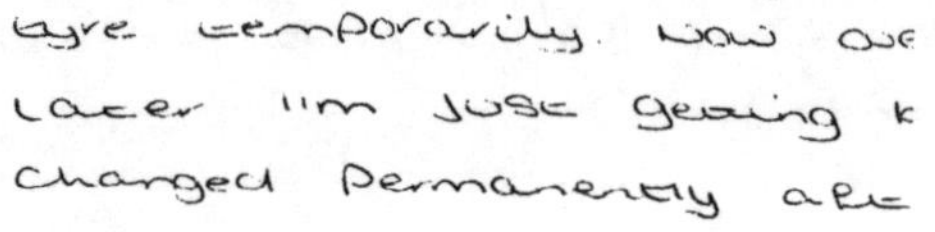

fig 9

Angular and Thread

Angular handwriting often has traces of thread connections within its framework (see fig. 10). The writer will be direct, abrupt and aggressive. In some cases, such a writer is downright rude and exhibits very little emotional consideration for anybody. He is intelligent and decisive and, unless you set out to upset him never try to appeal to his emotions, always use facts.

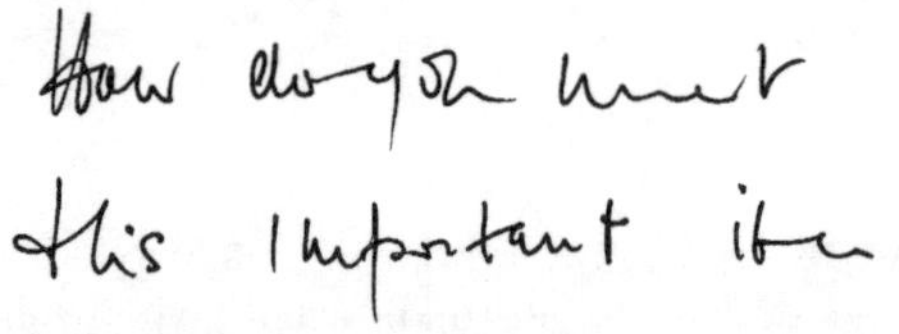

fig 10

To sum up, writing that is basically round with nice and easy flowing curves indicates that the writer is approachable, emotionally reasonable and fairly flexible. However, he is basically a follower. If you pose any threat to his personal security then anything goes when he defends himself. Writing that consists more of straight lines than curves implies energy and ambition, with a strong determination to win. There is a lot of spirit here for this writer is a natural leader, usually by example. Such a writer can be domineering at times but he is always full of enthusiasm to get the job done.

2
Handwriting Slant and Line Slope

Our early attempts at writing or drawing begin long before we go to nursery school and by the time we get to go to school proper, most of us know how to play and create with chalk, crayon, pen or pencil. Our individual abilities develop along with our contemporaries at much the same level once we do get into those early classes, and of course, once we are under the wing of our first teacher. However, there is still a very wide variety of first alphabets taught in primary schools. There is no 'national hand' as there is in other countries. The print-script system we learn (see fig. 1) is easy to assimilate and is a natural precursor to cursive handwriting.

fig 1
A B C D E F G H I J K L M N O P Q R
S T U V W X Y Z
abcdefghijklmnopqrstuvwxyz

As young children we develop our personal style from this basic alphabet. We modify our early attempts at writing largely to suit ourselves – teachers rarely insist that we write in a special style. As a result, we may introduce a twirl or curlicue here, delete a loop or two there, and slowly, steadily, adopt a style that suits us best.

The English national hand is written in a straight line across a page from left to right. When we reach the far edge of the paper we leave a small space below that line, start again and continue in the same way until we finish our missive. It is here, while still young and at this particular stage of our education that we tend to adopt a particular angle of handwriting to the base-line. Youngsters will develop either a slightly reclined or backward slant, an upright or vertical hand, or an inclined or forward slant.

Angle of slant

The slant we use at any one period can and does change. But over a period of time it tends to remain fairly constant. Whatever the adopted slant we use, certain personality traits are revealed (see fig. 2). The angle of writing we use normally is an outward expression of our real, inner feelings. This is an emotional response to our environment and the people with whom we associate. However, on some occasions there can be a measurable difference, often as the result of a quite recent upset. Of course, you can only detect this if you have several samples of the same hand.

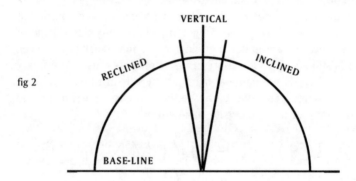

fig 2

VERTICAL
RECLINED
INCLINED
BASE-LINE

Reclined handwriting

Writing that slopes backward (see fig. 3)) is not taught anywhere in any school as part of the national curriculum, so it should be interpreted as an outward sign of a rebellious nature. The exception is the left-handed writer, whose writing almost always has a backward slant (see page 81). It is used by those right-handed people who are defiant, awkward and emotionally defensive. They lack natural spontaneity in their day-to-day dealings with other people. They are introverted and will hide their real feelings from everyone, including themselves, for they are not always as honest with themselves as they should be.

fig 3

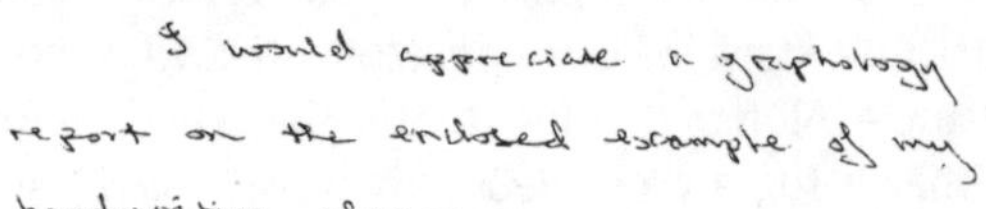

I would appreciate a graphology
report on the enclosed example of my
handwriting, please.

People who write like this are basically actors who present an outward show of calmness and control but want to be different. They feel all eyes are on them, and it is difficult for them to trust anyone. There will be few close and trusted friends, but there will be a wide circle of acquaintances from all walks of life. Extremely reclined handwriting (see fig. 4) suggests poor adaptability, with a lot of difficulty in expressing emotions physically. Such people are highly sensitive, prefer routine and regular lives, and will distrust anything new because it is new.

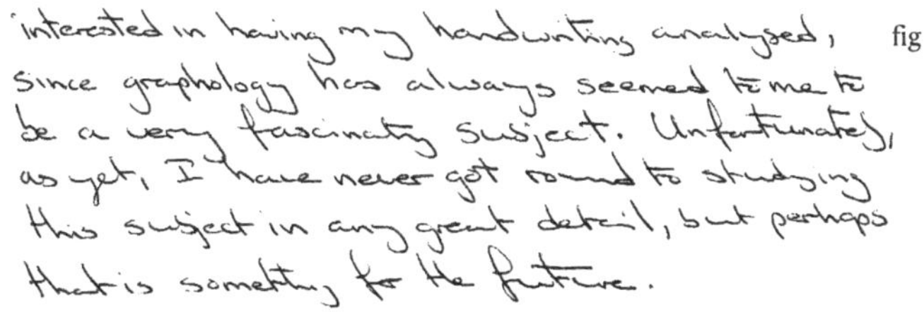

fig 4

Upright writing

Provided this writing is consistently upright (fig. 5) and only veers away from the vertical by no more than five degrees or so, it is fairly safe to assume the writer has a head-over-heart attitude to just about everything and everyone.

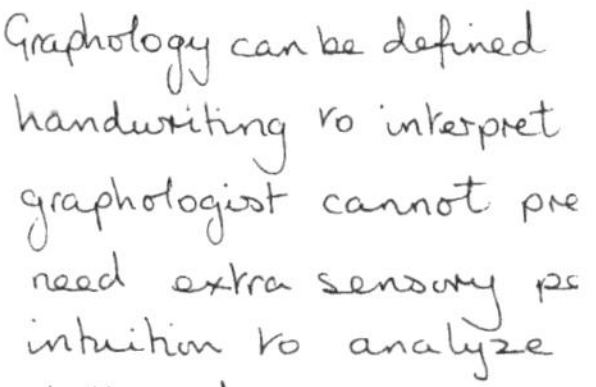

fig 5

Mostly, these writers are open to the mood of the moment and tend to be very cautious in their responses because feelings are kept very much under control at all times. Judgment is always a considered affair. However, in emergencies these people really shine and can be relied upon to keep their heads. There are always signs of control and caution but, if this is lost at any time, every effort is made to restore the status quo as soon as possible. Decisions are made on facts, not emotions. Overall, the impression these people give is one of independence, detachment or even indifference in some cases.

If the script is slightly reclined by about five degrees or more, the writer will exhibit caution and be very careful with other people, especially any new faces in their circle.

If, however, the writing inclines with a slightly forward slant, again, by no more than five degrees or so from the vertical (see fig. 6), the writer is more prone to action, open and sociable with a little less logic but a little more sympathy and warmth. This style is often seen in those who hold positions of authority. These writers are rarely over-demonstrative and tend to stay cool, calm, collected and confident – especially in crises.

fig 6

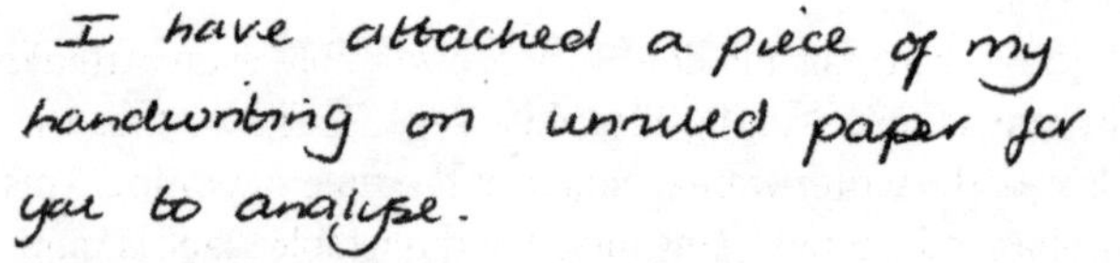

I have attached a piece of my handwriting on unruled paper for you to analyse.

If the forward angle is greater than this (see fig. 7) there is more impulse in their nature, and they thrive happily on variety and change. These writers bluff well and often gives a false impression of confidence. Feelings will be much stronger and more freely demonstrated. Decision-making is more emotionally based. Some writers tend to be chameleon-like and take on the mood of the moment, being openly compassionate and able to identify. There is an inclination to stay in an undemanding job or career. The less effort or energy needed the better.

fig 7

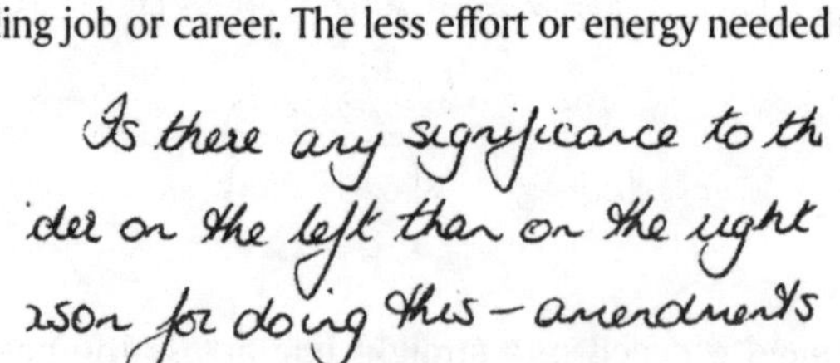

*Is there any significance to th
der on the left than on the right
ison for doing this – amendments
thou distracting the eye as occ*

Extremely inclined handwriting (see fig. 8) reflects volcanic emotions, up one minute and down the next. Writers like this are so responsive and ardent they are more likely to fall in love with love than the actual person to whom they have been suddenly attracted. These people are very susceptible to outside influences and are very easily sidetracked. They are also unsettled, restless and easily moved to love or hate with equal intensity.

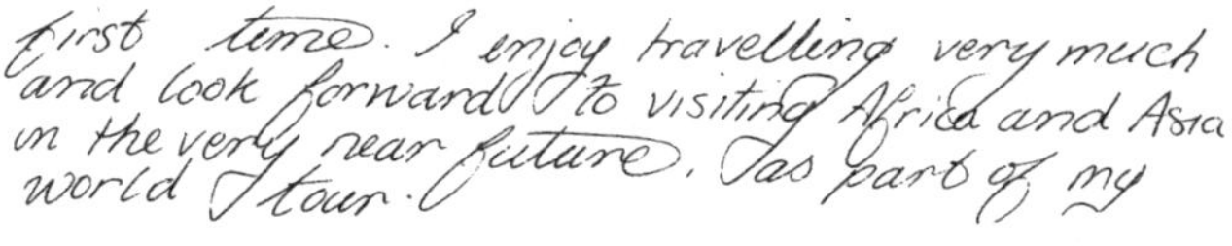

fig 8

As a rule, most handwriting slants stay much the same throughout life, and what small variations do occur may be considered normal up to about five degrees either way, indicating good personal control by the writer.

Mixed slant

Handwriting slant can and does vary considerably, even within the same line in one sample (see fig 9). When seen, it shows that the natural impulses of the writer were unstable at the time of writing. This cannot be emphasized enough. This mixed and unstable slant is quite consistent with unsettled characters who are much concerned with the mood of the moment. As they are basically insecure, these writers experience mood swings to such an extent that their overall emotional nature is quite erratic. They are undisciplined and capricious, and cannot be trusted to keep cool when needed. They lack balanced judgment and common sense and are often predictably unpredictable.

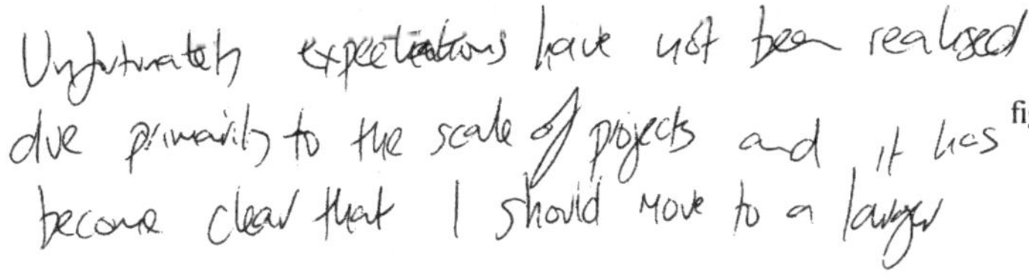

fig 9

Line slope

Writing should proceed in a straight line across the page and any variations in the line slope will help indicate the disposition of a writer at the time of writing. This is one of the reasons why we prefer to have our samples written on plain, unlined paper.

The base-line should hold steady across the page in a reasonably straight line. When it does so (see fig. 10 overleaf), it reveals good outward personal control, a smooth inner composure, overall order and discipline and reliability. Generally speaking, one should expect

fig 10

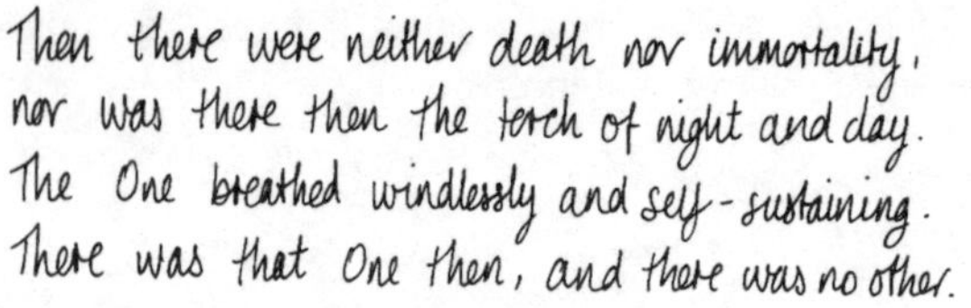

> Then there were neither death nor immortality,
> nor was there then the torch of night and day.
> The One breathed windlessly and self-sustaining.
> There was that One then, and there was no other.

these writers to exhibit good, steady responses to most external influences. These people will take things in their stride without too much stress or strain. But usually all writers tend to display some flexibility of the line flow.

When a line is too steady or has been written with a ruler under it, far too much control is being exerted in the writer's emotional and social dealings. He is afraid of being seen to lose control and any natural spontaneity is stilted. Quite often, there is a very strong element of narrow-mindedness.

Sometimes the handwriting begins on a level line but then arches upwards and descends again to the base-line (see fig. 11). This convex writing is a sign of initial confidence and enthusiasm for the project to hand, but the writer soon tires. Much gets started – but little is finished.

fig 11

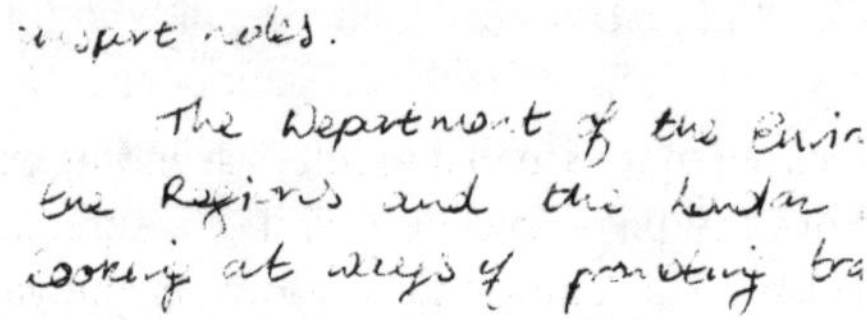

> import notes.
>
> The Department of the Envir
> the Regions and the Lender
> looking at ways of providing tra

The opposite of this is concave handwriting (see fig. 12), where the line dips downwards but eventually rises up again to the base-line. This is when the writer starts well enough but loses interest, or lacks confidence in his own ability. He then seems to rally, and comes back to finish in a far better frame of mind.

fig 12

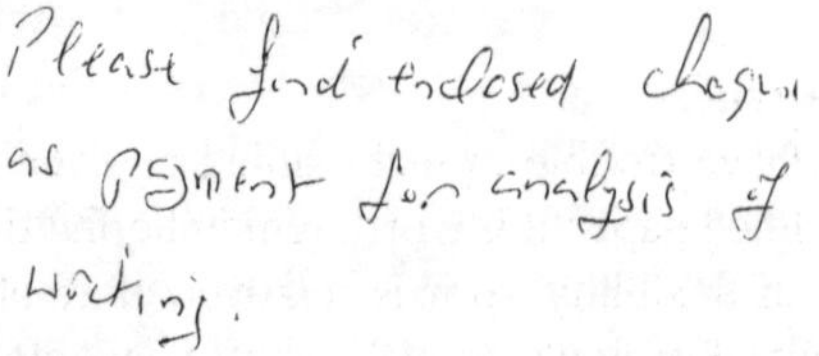

> Please find enclosed chequ
> as payment for analysis of
> writing.

Wavy baselines (see fig. 13) imply a strong response to outside influences. These writers can be easily side-tracked, their energy is

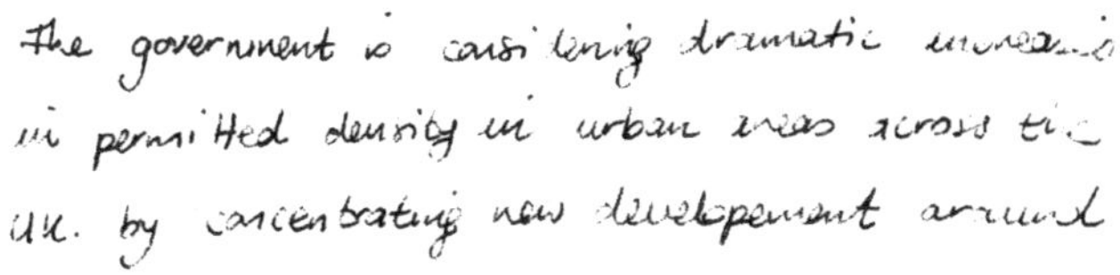

The government is considering dramatic increase in permitted density in urban areas across the UK. by concentrating new development around

fig 13

poorly channelled, talents go to waste and they are not very reliable.

Lines can start level but then fall away (see fig. 14). This often appears in handwriting when the writer is simply tired or has been overdoing it. After a good meal and adequate rest, the natural handwriting re-appears. However, lines can fall away for other reasons. The writer may be feeling apathetic or despondent because of some recent bad news, a disagreement or similar problems that have affected him emotionally.

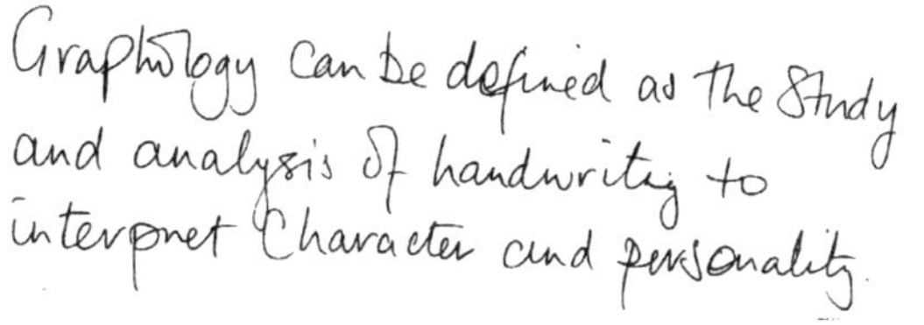

Graphology can be defined as the study and analysis of handwriting to interpret character and personality.

fig 14

When the lines seem to rise in a regular ascending pattern as the writing goes across the page (see fig. 15) it is a sure sign of enthusiasm and optimism. The emotional outlook is buoyant and very little gets this writer down: he has an inbuilt resilience to setbacks.

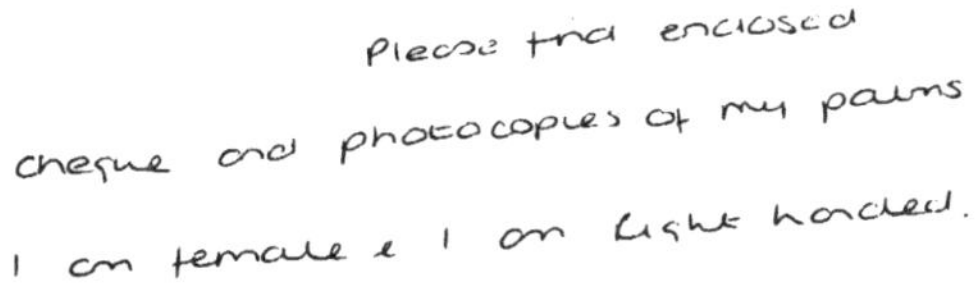

Please find enclosed cheque and photocopies of my palms 1 am female & 1 am light handed.

fig 15

General appearance

Some writers have trouble in maintaining an even flow even when they write on lined paper. It is worth remembering that all of us show some degree of flexibility, so it is relatively normal and not always that important. But look at the whole page for further clues. Compare the end of the page or letter with the beginning. We all start our letters with some degree of care, but as we progress and become caught up with what we want to say, our attention to convention slips.

Sometimes, there will be several attempts to return to a writer's initial standard, where he has paused to consider the next part of his message. This almost always reveals someone who does care and tries to maintain an even approach. In such a case, it follows that the writer is a responsible and thoughtful person irrespective of the overall style. He does try to pay some attention to detail. Just how much will be defined by the degree of changes in the base-line in the whole letter.

3

Layout, Size and Spacing

Layout

Take a sheet of A4 paper, fold it once lengthwise and once along the other edge. When you reopen it there will be four equal areas, each of which has a bearing on the character and personality of the writer once he has written on it.

The top half of the paper represents the future, the ambitions and hopes of the writer. The bottom half shows how we normally relate to the material things of life, our possessions, instincts and sexual drive.

The left-hand side represents the past, the ego and our memories. The right-hand side is said to be the way we view the future, our initiative and activity levels.

When we divide the paper into four areas like this we are able to establish the overall attitude of the writer to other people and his immediate environment. The way the writer uses space on the page is a fair barometer of his general social approach and general behaviour patterns.

The more the writing occupies the top half of the paper the more the writer will exhibit idealism, but may well lack objectivity. He may be over-informal and lack respect for the addressee, or be indifferent. If the writing fills the bottom of a page it suggests a largely practical nature and materialism. There will also be a strong streak of acquisition to go with it. This writer is also likely to be impulsive.

Writing on the left-hand side of the page indicates introversion and some timidity – the past holds more than the future for those who write like this. When the right-hand side is more favoured, the writer will have extrovert tendencies with plenty of on-the-surface self-confidence and initiative: he can bluff well.

Writing placed neatly in the centre of the paper (see fig. 1 overleaf) shows order and precision. However, the writer is likely to be slightly withdrawn and difficult to get to know. He will be rather conventional and know the difference between right and wrong.

Thus, just opening a letter and viewing how the writing is placed on the page immediately reveals certain personality foibles that will, of course, be confirmed or otherwise with other features in the rest of the script.

fig 1

fig 2

fig 3

fig 4

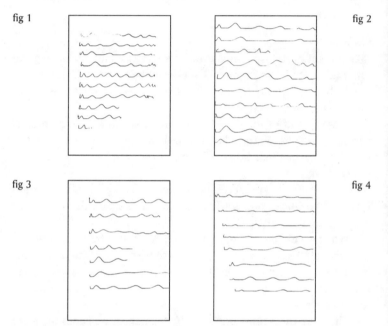

Margins

The writer's attention, or otherwise, to margins can show other personality characteristics. When margins are small or not present at all (fig. 2), the writer is overly concerned with getting his message over, at any cost. He does not plan well and is quite talkative. There will be a lazy streak but he means well.

If there is a wide left-hand margin (see fig. 3), the writer is over-friendly and extravagant with resources. An adept at wasting time, he is also superficially extrovert and may lack taste in some areas. A left-hand margin that becomes progressively wider down the page (fig. 4) shows impatience and optimism. Money comes and goes with an equal facility. Ambitions are marked but the writer lacks the ability to organize and plan.

If the left-hand margin narrows as the writing progresses (fig. 5), there will be distrust, innate caution and perhaps an inability to let go of the past. A lack of confidence associated with the subject matter, or between the writer and the addressee, is also possible.

fig 5   fig 6

fig 7   fig 8

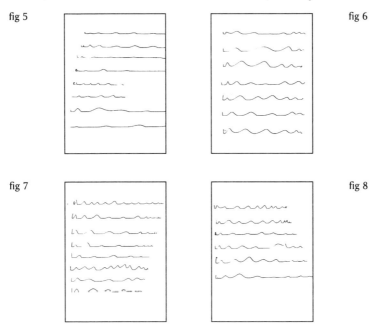

A wide right-hand margin (fig. 6) means that the writer fears the future, is sensitive and lacks spontaneity. Relationships are difficult to maintain, and the writer is too self-conscious, restless and pessimistic. If the margin widens as the writing continues down the page (fig. 7) it implies shyness and an inner reserve difficult to overcome. There is a fear of the future and self-confidence will be poor.

A narrow right-hand margin (fig. 8) shows that this writer means well to start with, but allows his impulses to take over. His initial shyness quickly vanishes because while he is a naturally friendly type and very easy to get along with, he may not take kindly to too much early familiarity.

When both left-hand and right-hand margins are uneven (see fig. 9) the writer will prove unreliable in certain circumstances and will eventually display a rebel streak or be plain awkward as the mood takes him. An irregular left-hand margin is a sign of poor control. The writer will exhibit self-defensiveness or protectiveness when challenged over an issue. His lack of self-confidence will be the measure of how much this is so. He may also lack initiative.

fig 9   fig 10

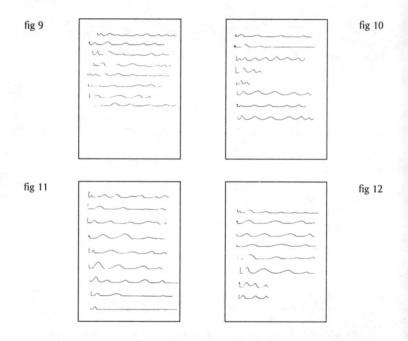

fig 11   fig 12

A poor right-hand margin is more the norm. If what is written has created an uneven margin for reasons of grammar, the writer shows some semblance of control. However, if this is not the case, then he exercises poor planning ability and judgment.

If the bottom margin is wide (see fig. 10), the writer is reserved or cautious in all his relationships. He is distrustful where others are concerned and may have sexual problems. There will be few real friends and not many acquaintances either. A narrow margin at the bottom of the paper (see fig. 11) shows over-concern with material matters. There is a strong emphasis on the physical and more mundane issues. The writer could be sensual and selfish. He might have a collecting hobby.

A wide top margin (see fig. 12) is probably meant as a mark of respect, for it is how a formal letter should be started. This is the traditional manner as taught in school and comes naturally with us into adulthood. A narrow top margin (fig. 13) shows poor planning, and a lack of respect for convention and common courtesy. The writer will be overly informal and there may be some aggression in the way he approaches others. He is likely to have an inferiority complex.

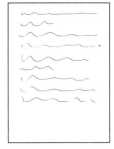

fig 13

These guidelines may be emphasized by the style of handwriting, slant, slope, and connections. Good writing with poorly planned margins means something quite different from low-level script that features good margins. Check for pressure, speed and spacing in the handwriting before making final decisions.

Size of handwriting

The size and spacing of writing relates to the way in which the writer wants to be seen by others. His sense of personal esteem will be shown by the size of his script. But the way he feels he ought to fit in, rather than actually does, is reflected in the way he uses space.

People who write an average, normal-size handwriting (see fig. 14) with little or no variation are conventional, practical and realistic. These people fit in easily everywhere because they are so adaptable. They strike a happy medium between what is right and wrong with equal facility. They do not make too much fuss whatever the task at hand – they just get on with it.

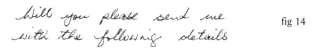

fig 14

Those who adopt a large script (see fig. 15 overleaf) want to be the centre of attention and make an impression all the time. They like to be recognized, dislike their own company, and much prefer to be with others as often as possible. Basically, large writing implies an expansive nature, someone who is always restless and lacks the ability to concentrate. He is often selfish, ostentatious, and loves display and grandeur.

fig 15

Those who pen a small script (see fig. 16) are able to concentrate, often for long periods at a time. They love detail, facts and figures and will approach all their tasks in a meticulous fashion. These people are rarely aggressive, and prefer to work in the background because they tend to dislike too much limelight. They are likely to be on the shy side, but they are also perceptive, original and very objective when they have to be. Just occasionally, those who write in this style may be independent and quite calculating, with a strong inner power drive.

fig 16

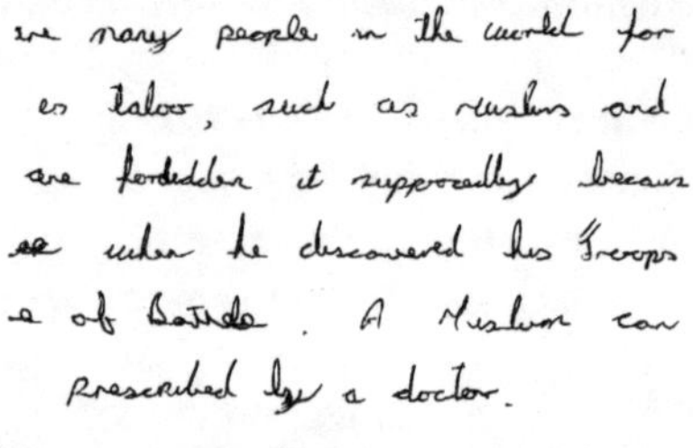

Those who write with variable letter sizes (see fig. 17) are often emotionally unstable, especially at the time of writing. As such, they are often unable to concentrate properly for any length of time. These writers are also self-centred and moody, and very responsive to the prevailing mood of the moment. They seem to have changeable opinions; one minute all for an idea, the next minute against it. Often, this is coupled with a physically demonstrative nature, adopting a hail-fellow-well-met manner quite early on in life – but it is not always sincere.

fig 17

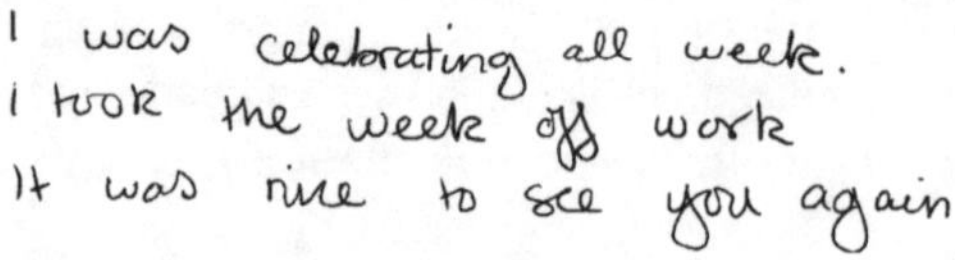

Horizontal expansion

Handwriting can be narrow, medium or wide and there is a simple test for assessing this. In medium-sized handwriting (see fig. 18) the letter n should look like a little square. If the n looks a little squeezed, like a vertical oblong, then the writing may be termed narrow. In a wide handwriting the letter n will look like a small oblong on its side.

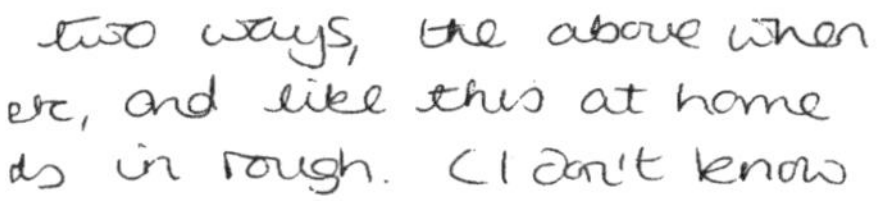

two ways, the above when etc, and like this at home ds in rough. <I don't know

fig 18

Medium-sized handwriting suggests the writer has inner contentment and, as a rule, is mostly well-balanced and flexible. Often, he has the ability to take charge, temporarily perhaps, but he has the happy knack of being able to size up the immediate problem and initiate positive action.

Narrow handwriting (fig. 19) suggests an inhibited nature. Such a writer will be inwardly insecure, have doubts about his own ability or worth and be slightly reserved. He is often reluctant to join in normal social life and may well be narrow-minded.

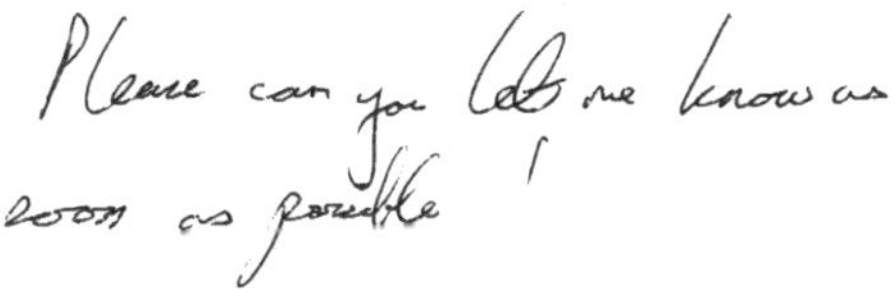

Please can you let me know as soon as possible

fig 19

Wide handwriting (fig. 20) indicates an expansive personality, an extrovert who cares little for the consideration of others and who is often selfish, especially if the writing is angular. People whose handwriting looks like this are a law unto themselves. Where others might bend the rules, these people either 'adapt' them or even break them if necessary.

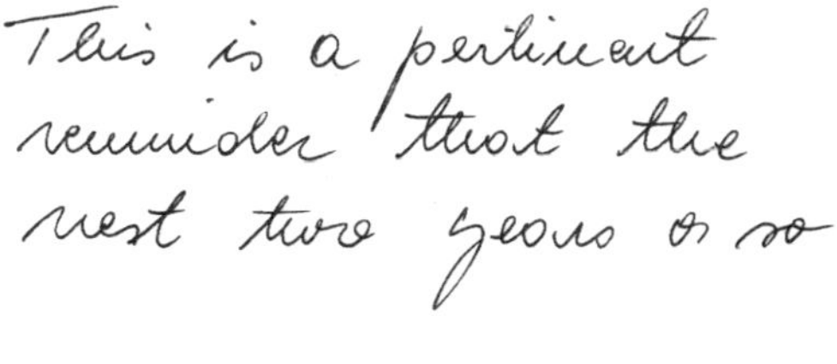

This is a pertinent reminder that the next two years or so

fig 20

Inconsistent horizontal size (see fig. 21) is often seen in the handwriting of young people around puberty. Obviously, this is a reflection of their ever-changing moods and attitudes because of all the many biological changes affecting their emotional reactions. However, when you see this style of handwriting in a more adult person, expect to find a rather mixed-up social nature. The script looks as though there is a (temporary) loss of form and reflects the writer's mood at the time of writing, for he too is very much influenced by the prevailing mood of the moment. He either does not, or will not, try to control his responses.

fig 21

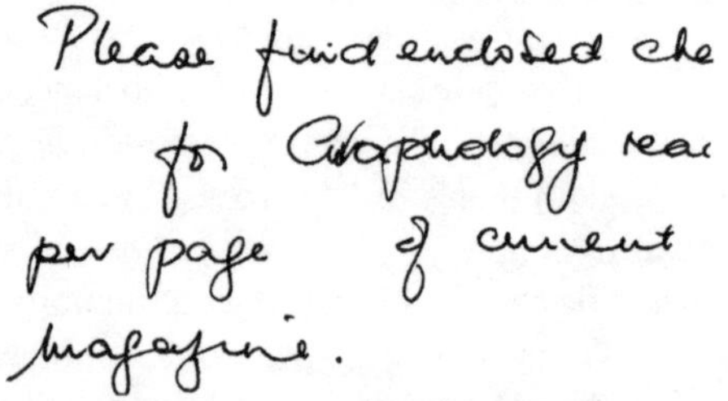

Spacing

In addition to the layout and size of handwriting you must also take into account the way in which a writer uses space on a page. Spacing between letters, words and lines show a writer's attitude to his relationships, environment and general sociability. From the way the writer uses space we are able to assess the quality of restraint, objectivity and tolerance present. It is also possible to detect if the writer is companionable, narrow-minded or bigoted.

Good, clear, well-balanced spacing (see fig. 22) between individual letters, words and lines shows consistent and constructive thinking, an organized mind and good judgment.

fig 22

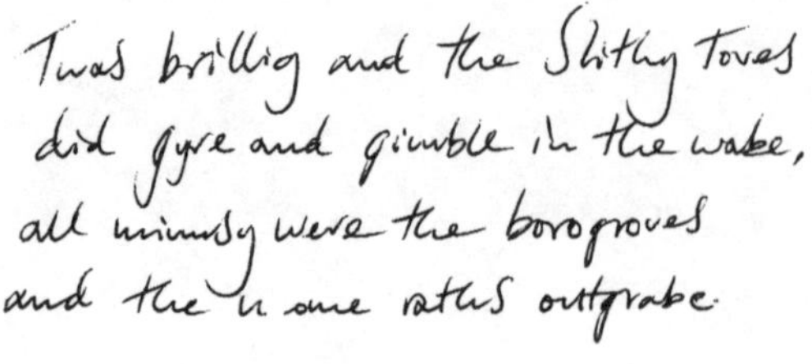

Spacing between letters

Spacing between letters indicates the real, innermost thoughts and ideals of the writer, of how he feels inside and relates to those around him.

When a writer squeezes his letters together (fig. 23) they may often look taller than they are wide. These people want close relationships but may be unable to express themselves properly.

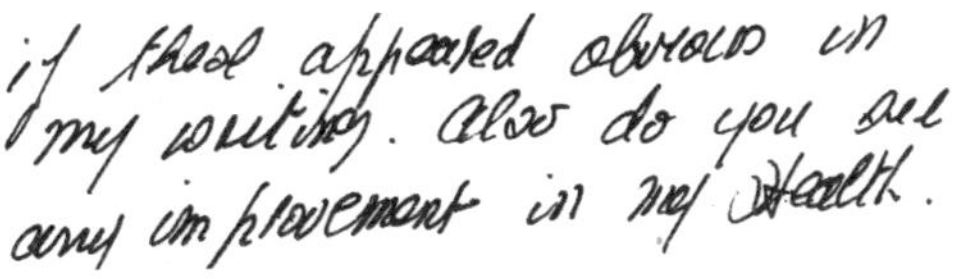

fig 23

When letters are moderately well spaced (fig. 24), the writer has a good social sense and mixes well. He stands on his own two feet and is well able to take advantage of a situation if or when he sees the right opening.

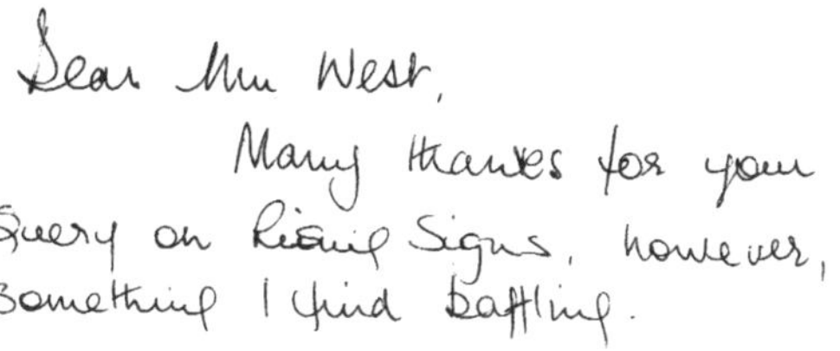

fig 24

If individual letters seem wide in themselves and the spacing between them is also wide (see fig. 25), it suggests an outgoing, extrovert personality.

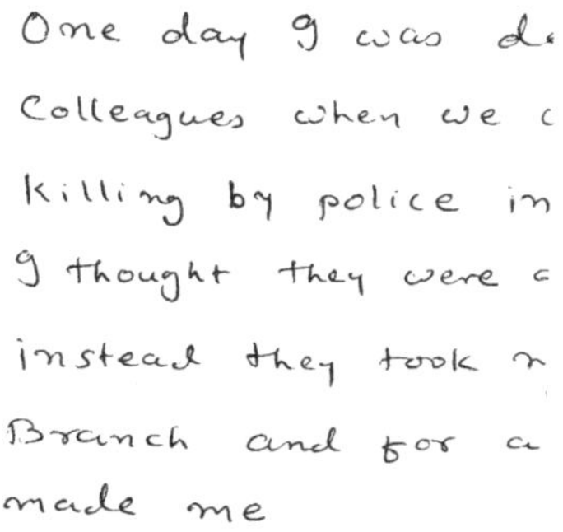

fig 25

37

Spacing between words

Spacing between words reveals the way in which the writer relates to others and is an indication of how well he uses his social skills.

If the spaces between words seem narrow (see fig. 26) or the words even seem to overlap at times, the writer is selfish and puts himself in the forefront at all times. This also suggests an independent nature.

fig 26

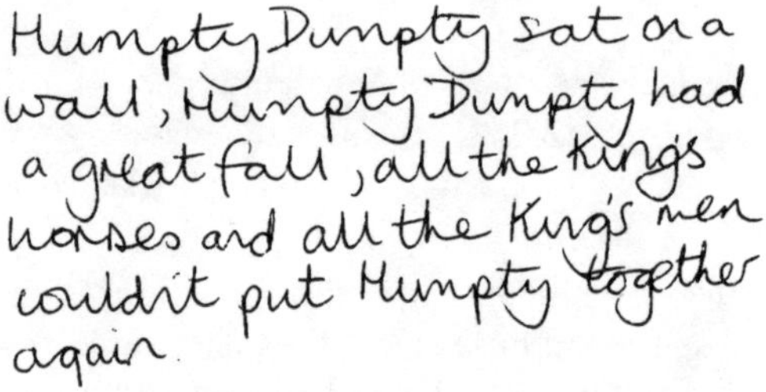

> Humpty Dumpty sat on a
> wall, Humpty Dumpty had
> a great fall, all the Kings
> horses and all the King's men
> couldn't put Humpty together
> again.

A medium spacing between words (see fig. 27) shows good social sense. This is a reasonably independent type who can give as good as he gets when dealing with other people, collectively or singly.

fig 27

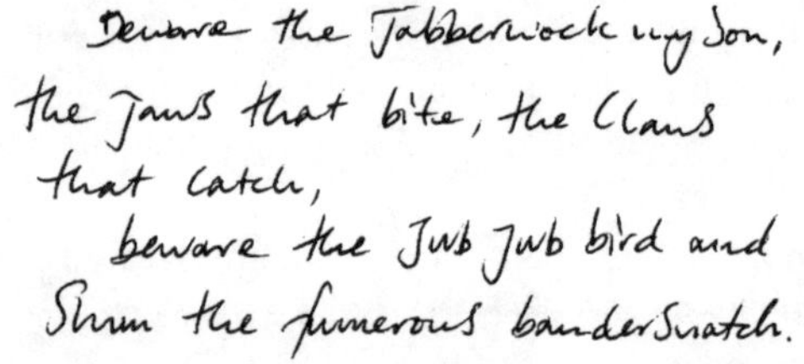

> Beware the Jabberwock my son,
> the jaws that bite, the claws
> that catch,
> beware the Jub Jub bird and
> Shun the frumerous banderSnatch.

Wide spaces between words (fig. 28) are unmistakable and show a writer who prefers to keep himself to himself. He protects his privacy, may seem aloof or unapproachable and acts with restraint.

fig 28

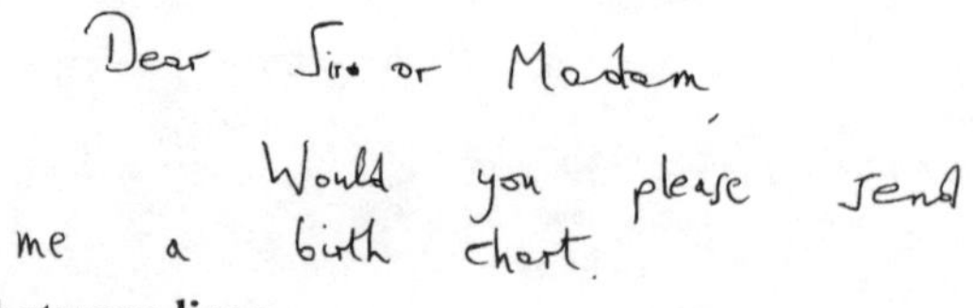

> Dear   Sir or Madam,
>
> Would   you   please   send
> me   a   birth   chart.

Spacing between lines

When lines are spaced in such a way that lower loops tangle with the upper loops of the line below (see fig. 29) it suggests a liking for good social contact, but there is too much inner confusion. Thinking may be muddled and the writer can appear self-defensive if challenged.

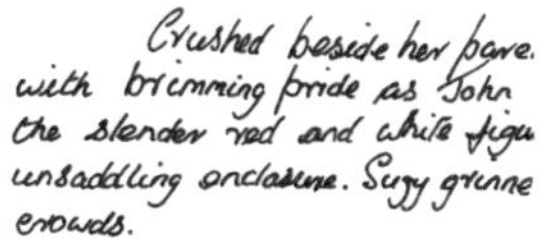

Crushed beside her bare.
with brimming pride as John
the slender red and white figu
unsaddling onclaseme. Surg grinne
crowds.

fig 29

A medium space between lines (fig. 30) shows that the writer enjoys a good healthy social life and is known for his moderate views and independence – up to a point. He will be reasonably flexible and happy to go along with the crowd.

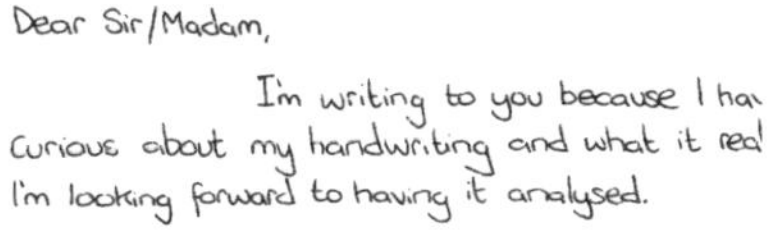

Dear Sir/Madam,

I'm writing to you because I ha
Curious about my handwriting and what it real
I'm looking forward to having it analysed.

fig 30

The greater the space between lines (fig. 31) the more privacy the writer feels he must have. He has a fear of too much close contact, and needs to feel free and unfettered by obligations he may not always understand. It is possible that he may have been hurt in the past and the memory still lingers.

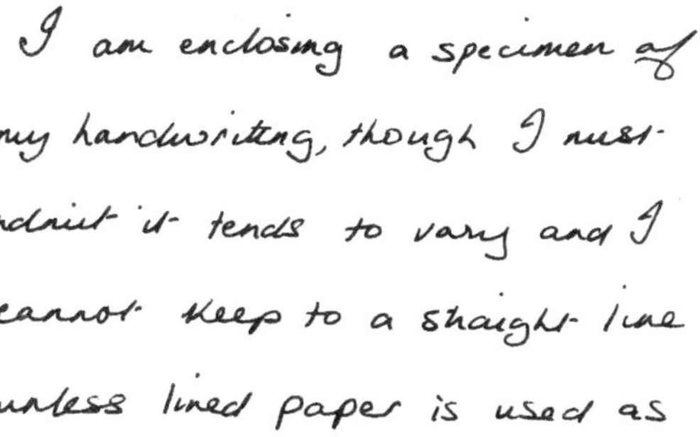

I am enclosing a specimen of
my handwriting, though I must
admit it tends to vary and I
cannot keep to a straight line
unless lined paper is used as

fig 31

4

Handwriting Zones

Handwriting is divided into three vertical zones or areas, each of which should be no more than about three mm ($^1/_4$-inch) high (see fig. 1). Handwriting that is consistently larger than this may be termed large, and any zones that consistently appear less than three millimetres should be considered as small. These three zones can be interpreted in terms of time and space as outlined many years ago by Sigmund Freud.

The upper zone represents the future, the middle zone the present and the lower zone the past. In terms of spatial analogy we may say the upper zone represents the head; the middle zone, the trunk; and the lower zone, the lower body and legs.

fig 1

| UPPER |
| MIDDLE |
| LOWER |

Thus the way the upper zone is constructed reflects the writer's aspirations, ambitions, beliefs, and general perceptivity. Should any irregularities appear in the upper zone they might reflect a mental and/or physical problem in this area. For example, there may be a series of consistent broken loops in one sample that do not appear in another example from the same source. At the time of writing the writer may have had a severe headache, had injured a part of his upper body, bumped his head, or something of a similar nature had occurred. In all others aspects, the way the upper zone is constructed will represent the writer's basic aims.

The way the middle zone is created indicates a writer's personal thoughts on his immediate environment, and the way he projects himself when associating with the people in it. Any irregularity in the middle zone may be relevant to problems in the trunk of the body. The way the middle zone is constructed represents a writer's ego.

The way the writer creates his lower zones reveals his basic, natural instincts, sexual urges, his love of possessions, the way he may acquire them, and his general materialism. If there are any inconsistencies here it suggests problems associated with the lower part of the body.

The style in which the writer proportions these zones is directly associated with his ability to balance his life style within the parameters of the zones and, of course, what they represent. Each letter of the alphabet occupies one or more zones and, in doing so, assumes a greater or lesser importance dependent on how it is individually penned and whether or not it invades a zone to which it does not belong.

Of course, the exception to zonal invasion is the letter f – the only tri-zonal letter. This should always extend from the upper zone, through the middle and into the lower zone. Naturally, how it is individually constructed must also be taken into account.

The upper zone letters are b, d, f, h, k, l, t and the lower case i because of the dot. Each of these letters also occupies a part of the middle zone. When you assess the way they are constructed in the upper zone you must remember to look at the way they are written in the middle zone as well.

The middle zone letters are a, c, e, m, n, o, r, s, u, v, w and x. Each of these letters is solely to be found (normally) in the middle zone. However, writers can and often do create upper or lower zone extensions for some of them. It is essential to take such extra ticks, loops, or other marks into account.

The lower zone letters are g, j, p, q, y and z. Each of these letters also occupies a part of the middle zone. When you assess the way they are constructed in the lower zone you must remember to look at the way they are written in the middle zone as well.

When all three zones are reasonably well-balanced, mostly all the same size and construction, the writer has a good, healthy ego, is relatively stable and gets on quite well with his peers.

It is very important to remember that when one or more zones are emphasized in any way the remainder will *always* be off-balance, especially if a letter should enter a zone with which it may not normally be associated. When one zone is exaggerated or over-developed in such a way as to encroach into one or both of the other

41

two zones, an element of distortion or confusion will be observable in the writer's sense of proportion within the zones involved. Any disproportionate imbalance between the zones will represent either the writer's over-enthusiasm or concern within that zone.

Thus, an over-proportioned upper zone (fig. 2), with high-reaching loops and stems that tend to dwarf the middle and lower zones suggests a highly ambitious nature, plenty of intelligence, a dreamer and an idealist. However, there will also be a lack of maturity and a lack of practical, common sense.

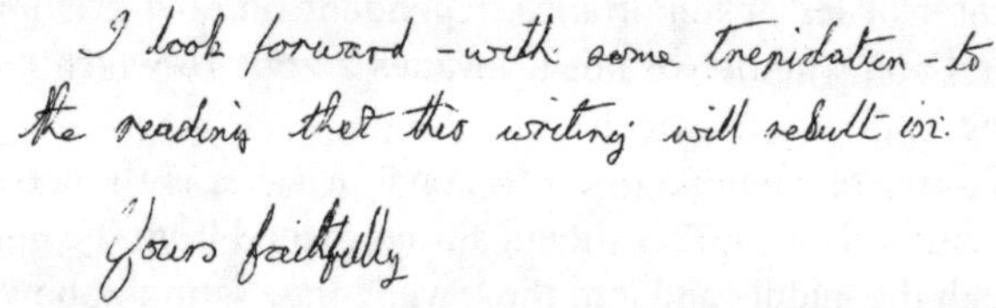

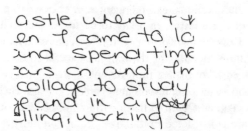

fig 2

An over-proportioned middle zone (fig. 3) that dwarfs the upper and lower zones implies a selfish character, one more concerned about his own world to the exclusion of almost all else. He will almost certainly be conceited, presumptuous or seemingly uncaring of the plight of others, especially if he is a leader of some kind. Such a writer is easily bored – and can be boring too.

fig 3

An over-proportioned lower zone (fig. 4 overleaf), with long down-reaching loops or descenders that seem to dwarf the middle and upper zones and make them look small by comparison indicates strong over-concern with physical and material pleasures. The writer must experience all things at first hand; the constant stimulation of change has a very high priority. This writer will always want to feel secure; his needs between this and his strong desire for variety will cause inner, emotional problems.

in gave each other nickna
with young. Ricky, for som
cure to mere adults was
siblings and Matthew,(
s MATT) who had instiga
g was lovingly called
(after the retarded fellou

A small upper zone (see fig. 5), with loops or ascenders reaching only a tiny way above the middle zone suggests the writer lacks ambition and the drive to succeed. As a rule, this type is usually practical and reliable, quite realistic but not always very creative.

this subject, any beginner based
I am
recommend would be appreciated, o.
a home study course, especialey

In a handwriting where the middle zone has hardly any ascenders or descenders extending into the upper or lower zones (see fig. 6), expect the writer to under-rate himself and his abilities. He starts with a negative attitude that rarely changes; he is also likely to have an inferiority complex. He can be very creative, but may lack sufficient push to resolve things constructively. A very small zone is an indication of a mind well able to concentrate for long periods at a time. This writer often has a strong independent streak.

I would be grateful if
prepare for me 6 mon
My date of birth is 16
I enclose cheque for £:

An under-emphasized lower zone (see fig. 7), with small loops and ascenders that only just reach a tiny way below the middle zone suggests a lack of drive and interest in all the physical aspects of life. The writer will probably have a low sex drive and not be over bothered about his general comforts. As a rule, this writer seems to be

43

quite content to drift about his daily round rather than push for anything better with any perceptible level of effort unless it is for a strongly desired aim.

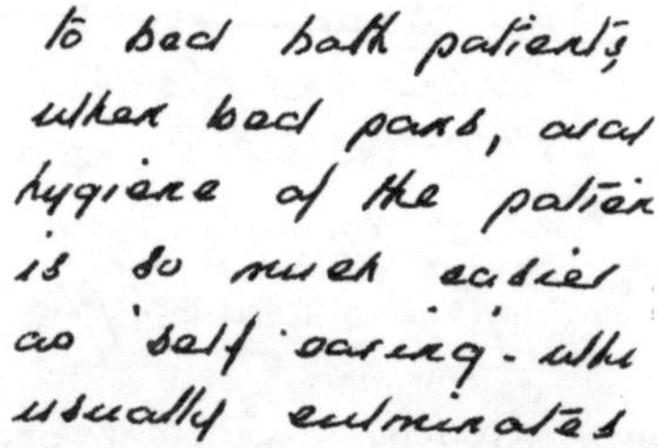

fig 7

If a variety of ascenders are in evidence (see fig. 8), loops, heavy upward strokes, stick-like lines, or even the occasional absence of any line into the upper zone when there should be one, it indicates a changeable nature where the writer's ideals and ambitions are concerned. When there are changes or different accentuations in the upper zone it always indicates the writer's inability to plan or even act in a consistent manner when pursuing his aims. It is a mark of the dreamer who just cannot or will not get his act together: he is very easily side-tracked.

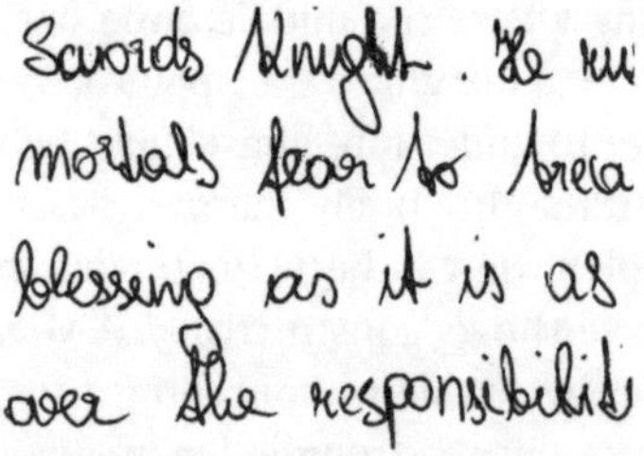

fig 8

When there are a variety of descenders, loops, heavy downward strokes, stick-like lines, even an occasional absence of a tail (fig. 9), it indicates an inconsistency of approach in day-to-day matters. Excessive changes or different accentuations in the lower zone is a sign of the writer's inability to act rationally or to respond properly. This writer is also easily side-tracked, especially if in the pursuit of pleasure.

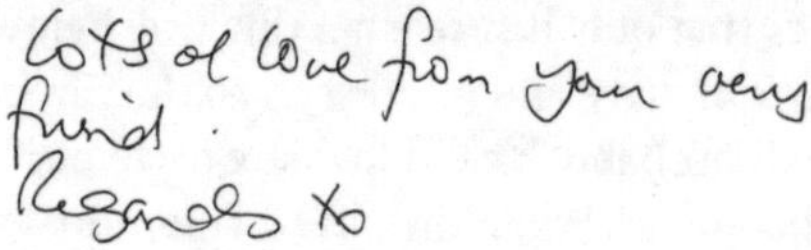

fig 9

5

Pressure and Speed

Now that the relative interpretations of size, spacing and zones of handwriting have been explained, we can show how to qualify and moderate these meanings in terms of pressure and speed of handwriting.

The pressure used by a writer indicates the physical energy and vitality available to him at the time of writing. Obviously, we must expect that the robust, athletic type will write in quite a different style to that of a more delicate and sensitive type. The athlete would certainly show his energies and write with a heavy hand. Those who are less active will exhibit a much more relaxed or light style.

Normally, one can detect heavy pressure either by sight or simply by feeling the back of the paper. Heavy pressure always shows plenty of energy, vitality and persistence. Handwriting pressure, like all other features, is a direct result of the writer's mood at the time of writing and not the type of writing instrument used.

When a writer uses a fountain pen the pressure exerted causes the split nib of the pen to bow or possibly separate according to the pressure he employs. As the pen moves across the paper in an even, slight pressure it will produce a line of uniform width. Heavy pressure makes the nib open and more ink is allowed through, thus making the line a much broader one. Light pressure shows as a thin line. While some people write in a smooth, even rhythmic style, others create shaky, halting or uneven lines of ink and between the two extremes there is a fairly wide variety of strokes.

The ballpoint is easily the most popular writing instrument today and, with heavy pressure the line it leaves can be a deep groove on the paper, often going right through to show on the reverse.

When a felt-tip or a pencil is used, the strength of the stroke may not be so apparent for, while the latter depends on a sharp point, the former needs a good supply of ink. In graphological analysis neither are very helpful in the assessment of pressure, but it can be detected with a little effort.

The lower down the barrel a pen is held, the more pressure may be applied, usually by the forefinger. The further up the barrel is held from the nib, any downward pressure is less likely to be as the result of the guiding hand. The weight of the hand or the movement of the arm assumes this responsibility.

Scrutiny under a strong magnifying glass shows a great difference between a strong firm stroke and one lightly traced. The former is clear-cut, while the latter is smooth and has a ragged outline.

A student graphologist should experiment by writing with as many different instruments as possible, using as many different papers and writing surfaces as possible. Remember, downstrokes are contracting strokes while upstrokes are release strokes. There is no substitute for the experience to be gained in this exercise. Where possible, compare your own handwriting, or that of a friend, or friends, using as many different combinations of pens and paper as possible. This extremely rewarding exercise will indicate the enormous differences that an individual pen or different type of paper will make to the personal style of any writer.

About fifty years or so ago most (older) people preferred to use their own fountain pen, but this has gradually died out as the ballpoint pen has taken precedence. It matters little who uses a biro but with a fountain pen it can and does make quite a difference to the 'set' of the nib. Recently, there has been a slight return to the use of the fountain pen. Whether this has anything to do with the modern upsurge of interest in graphology has yet to be discovered, but it does make analysis easier.

In any handwriting sample the pressure should be even from start to finish. If there is any variation at all it will probably be on the downstroke of some individual letters. If the pressure is heavy all the way through the script (see fig. 1), irrespective of direction, the writer will be a very physical type. He will be forceful, boastful, self-centred, critical and rather opinionated. His ambitions could all be in the wrong directions and not necessarily good for him. He often finds it difficult to relax, especially in company, and dislikes change.

When pressure is accentuated at the bottom of a downstroke the writer may have trouble in personal expression for, although basically inhibited he will be sexually preoccupied as well.

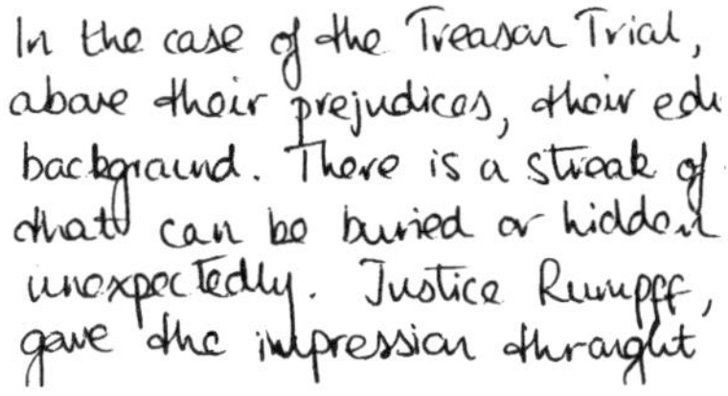

In the case of the Treason Trial,
above their prejudices, their edu
background. There is a streak of
that can be buried or hidden
unexpectedly. Justice Rumpff,
gave the impression throught

fig 1

If the pressure is at the top of an upstroke, it is a sign of inner anxiety. It is not natural for release strokes to be made heavily.

Pressure may show in horizontal or lateral strokes (see fig. 2), that is, in lead-in, connecting or ending strokes, or in dash-like i-dots or heavy t-bars. In such a case the writer will have anxiety problems, be unable to express his feelings properly, have unusual social behaviour patterns or exhibit an affectation of some kind.

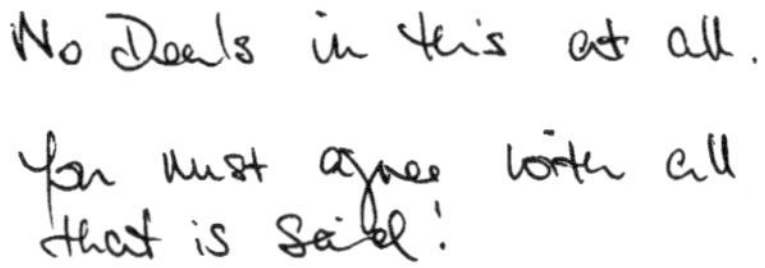

No Deals in this at all.

You must agree with all
that is said!

fig 2

Medium pressure (fig. 3) is the sign of a healthy mind in a healthy body. The writer has good willpower, is well-balanced emotionally, and has a fondness for life.

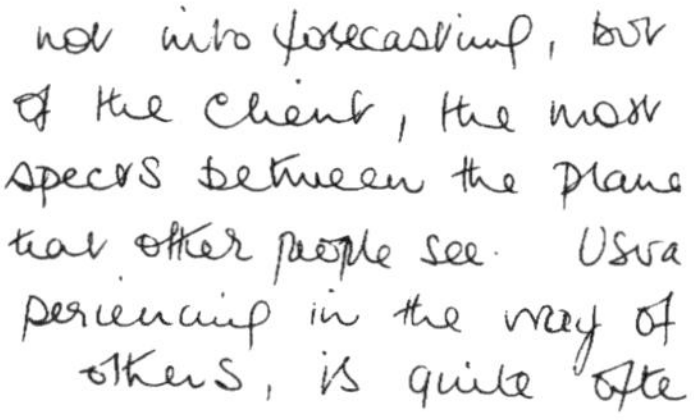

not into forecasting, but
of the client, the most
specks between the plane
tial other people see. Usva
periencing in the way of
others, is quite ofte

fig 3

Light, even pressure (see fig. 4 overleaf) means a more sensitive nature. The writer is sympathetic, understanding, reasonably flexible and often surprisingly perceptive. This type is usually quite strong mentally, dependent on other features in the writing, but may lack physical energy and vitality.

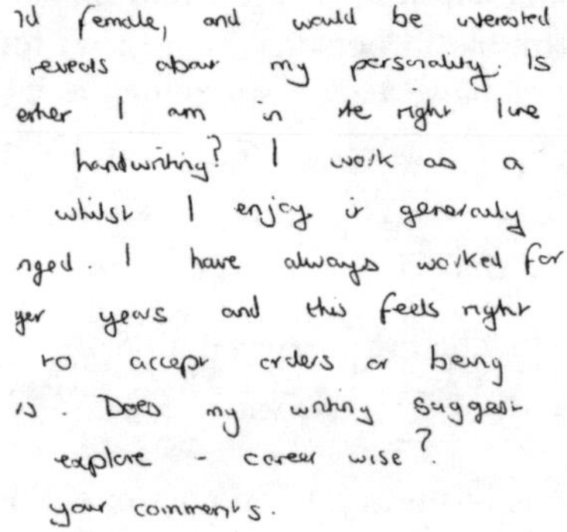

fig 4

[handwritten sample, fig 4:]

'd female, and would be interested
reveals about my personality. Is
either I am in the right line
handwriting? I work as a
whilst I enjoy it generally
good. I have always worked for
yer years and this feels right
to accept orders or being
is. Does my writing suggest
explore - career wise?
your comments.

Very light pressure (fig. 5) is always a sign of hypersensitivity, poor initiative and delicacy of feeling. Willpower is not strong, the writer tends to be rather tolerant and easy-going and yields to others very quickly. Peace at any price – almost.

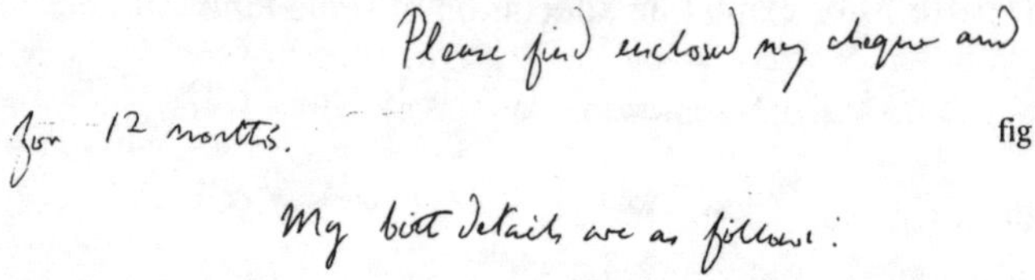

[handwritten sample, fig 5:]

Please find enclosed my cheque and
for 12 months.
My bank details are as follows:

fig 5

Uneven pressure (fig. 6) is a danger sign and suggests poor control at the time of writing. Perhaps some words may be more emphasized than others and if so, a check may show they are linked in some way. Here, the writer is instinctively stating preferences,

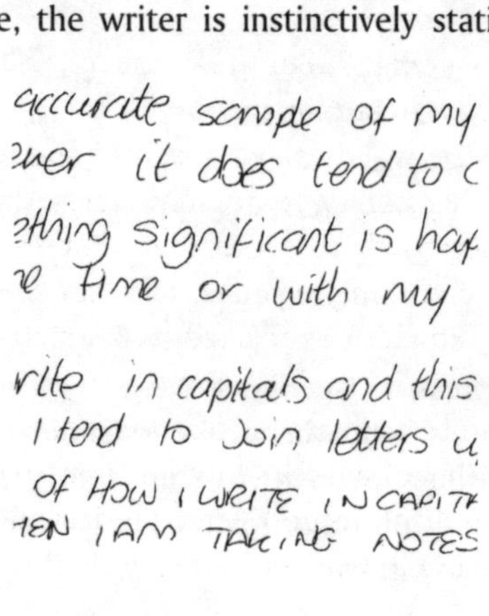

fig 6

[handwritten sample, fig 6:]

accurate sample of my
ever it does tend to c
ething significant is hap
e time or with my

rite in capitals and this
I tend to join letters u
OF HOW I WRITE IN CAPIT
TEN I AM TAKING NOTES

using his handwriting to pour out his troubles in such a way that the words are unconsciously stressed.

Many people claim that their handwriting is not always consistent and seems to change almost daily. All of us have moods – there are times when we are on top of the world and others when we might cheerfully strangle the first person who comes through the door. Some of us cope very well with these extremes, but others cannot. If you have just had a nasty few moments with the boss your mood and emotions will be very near the surface. If you were to take up your pen and write a few words there would be less control of your handwriting than normal. This is one way in which handwriting can reflect the emotional imbalance of a writer.

But if you had just enjoyed a day out with your favourite person or even spent a little time making love, then obviously your mood would be quite different. Your overall emotional control would be much more content. A letter written at this moment would reflect this, and if you were to have experienced both of these moods in one day your handwriting would show it. The pressure you use shows the physical, mental and emotional energy available at the time.

fig 7

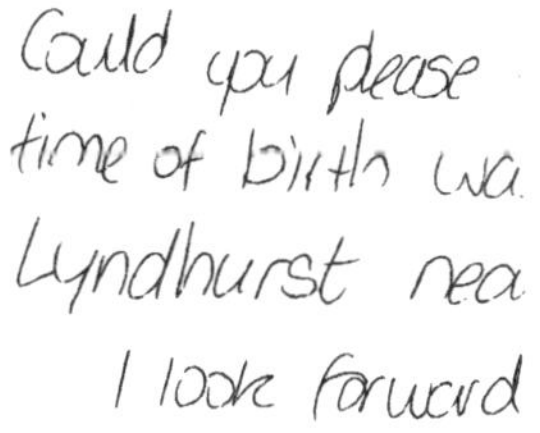

Width of stroke

Closely linked to pressure, but not always directly caused by it, is the width of the stroke in handwriting. There are four basic widths, thin, normal, thick or shaded.

Thin writing (see fig. 7) implies a certain amount of restraint in a writer's make-up. He will display a sensitive and refined approach to life and rely on his ability to reason things through rather than anything else. Often, these writers are super-efficient, pay little attention to the emotional niceties, and can seem cold by nature. They may find it difficult to socialize or be unable to relax properly in company.

Most writers use a normal stroke width, and when it is directly compared with a thin or a thick script it is easy to define. People who write in this style display good personal discipline and are reasonably conservative in the way they employ their personal energies.

49

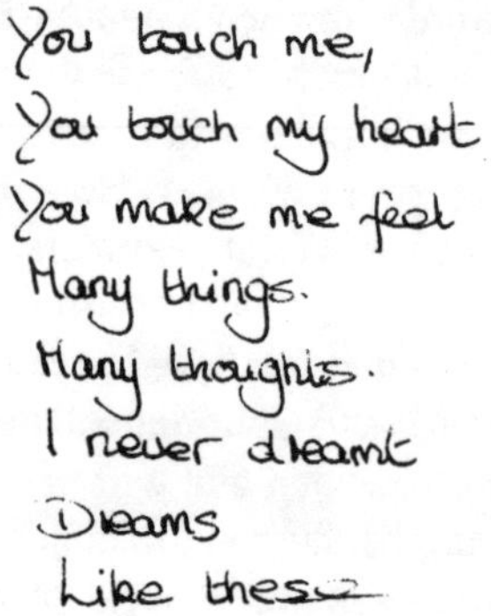

A thick writing stroke (fig. 8) denotes plenty of energy and vitality. This writer is sentimental and easily stirred emotionally. He likes the good things of life and relies a lot on his senses. Often this thick stroke suggests a sensuous nature, and those who write like this tend to rely on physical gratification of their senses more than may be good for them.

fig 8

> You touch me,
> You touch my heart
> You make me feel
> Many things.
> Many thoughts.
> I never dreamt
> Dreams
> Like these.

Shaded writing (fig. 9) is seen when both thin and thick lines appear in the same script and can be seen in both vertical and horizontal strokes. If this is seen with heavy pressure then the writer probably has artistic leanings and is someone to whom colour, light, shape and sound mean much. There are bound to be strong creative abilities present.

fig 9

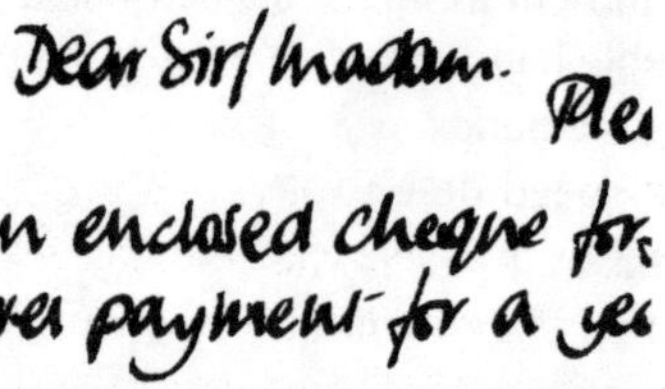

> Dear Sir/ Madam. Ple
> an enclosed cheque for
> over payment for a ye

Thus, the intensity of pressure indicates the amount of physical energy that is available to the writer, while the width of a line is concerned with how the writer may use that energy. The overall thinness or thickness of the handwriting shows how a writer prefers to experience that energy.

Speed

The speed of handwriting is linked with pressure and legibility. A script that is quite clear and readable does not necessarily give a clue to the mentality of the writer. As a rule, the speed of handwriting naturally increases with practice as the writer grows in confidence and reflects an ability to communicate. However, illegibility can imply a writer has something to hide. Speed will also show whether the writer is quick on the uptake or slow to perceive; the tempo shows how much natural spontaneity is present. Thus, speed indicates mental agility and energy. A fast writer thinks far more quickly than his slower counterpart who needs more time to get organized. Fast types do not always bother with conforming – they are too busy getting the message across.

The slow writer is different. He has to conform, he is aware that someone will have to read his writing and he will try to ensure that it is legible. In essence, this writer considers the reader, whereas the fast writer is not so concerned.

Curved handwriting, garland or arcade, is written more swiftly than straight or angular script. Punctuation marks such as a dot, comma or t-bar become stretched into dash-like marks – a sure sign of speed. Generally speaking, fast writing is inclined to the right while a slower script tends to be upright or may recline very slightly.

It is essential to remember that legibility does not necessarily mean intelligence: good, clear writing does not always mean good character, nor does poor legibility indicate a poor personality. Most people want to be understood, think clearly and are sincere, and will show this in a legible hand. However, it is quite unsafe to assume the reverse in an illegible hand.

Legibility and speed do not always go together, but when they do (see fig. 10) there is a sense of mental energy, perception and enthusiasm. The writer is objective, usually extrovert, rash and unreliable. He often makes very silly or avoidable mistakes and lacks an eye for detail: his concentration levels fluctuate, although this may depend on his interest in the subject matter. Legibility and speed often occur in writing only a step or two away from an original copybook style.

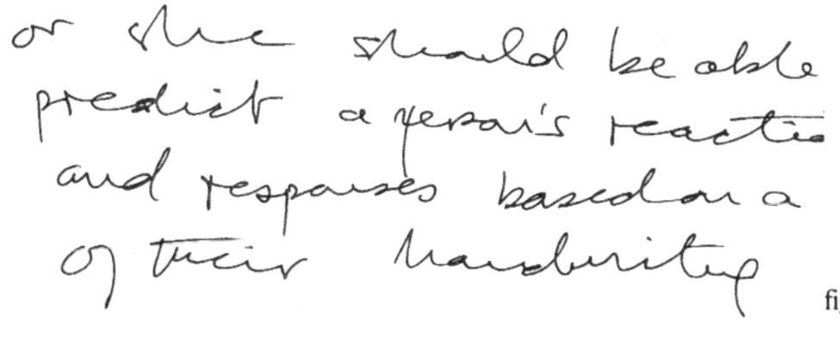

fig 10

51

The slow writer (see fig. 11) is steady, neat, reliable, and rather cautious. Often, the pace of a script can change as an individual word or series of words seem to be written slightly more slowly. This shows the writer has stopped to think about what to say next. He may have taken time to consider the reader and his reactions to what he is writing. Whether this is an emotional constraint, deference to the reader, or has another cause will be detected elsewhere.

fig 11

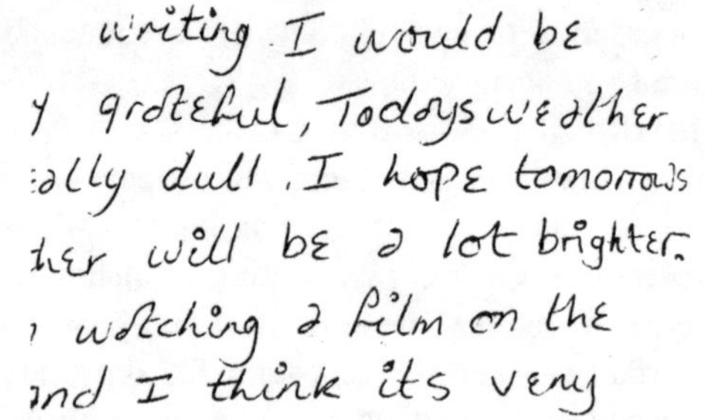

writing. I would be
y grateful, Todays weather
ally dull. I hope tomorrows
her will be a lot brighter.
, watching a film on the
and I think its very

Occasionally, especially when the emotional nature is aroused, the writer will emphasize certain words or phrases pertinent to the core of the message. The speed of the writing can increase or be written slightly higher or lower than the current base-line. Here, the writer is saying that he will get his message across no matter what the reader may think on receipt. Changes in pressure and speed become quite evident at such times and should be easily recognized. Vertical changes of pressure are an indication of a change of emotional temperament (release and control) while horizontal pressure implies anxiety, hysteria and an often misplaced self-assertion.

It helps to have a moderately powerful magnifying glass when you are about to examine handwriting for such details as pressure and speed. It is also helpful to have a watchmaker's eyeglass or a 'linen-prover' type of magnifying glass – usually readily available at most good opticians for a reasonable price.

6

Loops and Connections

Wherever they are found loops always indicate emotion, even when they appear where they might not normally be expected to be seen. To determine the quality and extent of expressed and or repressed emotion, look to the development or otherwise of the upper- and lower-zone loops.

The manner in which handwriting is connected indicates the amount of logic, inspiration and intuitional ability, but this specific part of analysis belongs more properly in the writing style and is dealt with more fully in that chapter.

When assessing the emotional factors in a full analysis it does help to also look at the development of reason and the amount of intuition that prevails.

Loops and strokes

Loops always indicate emotion, and this is measured by the amount of height, depth and width those loops achieve in relation to the middle zone. The more angular the appearance of the loop the more the writer will have some aggression in his nature. The rounder the writing, the more soft and yielding the approach. Pointed loops, whether in the upper or lower zone almost always refer to a rebel streak. Thus, a pointed upper loop suggests a radical or non-conforming thinker. A pointed lower loop reveals a writer with unusual basic instincts. Both writers have a temper.

Upper-zone loops and strokes.

In handwriting analysis, the upper zone represents the writer's mental and imaginative powers. Loops in the upper zone reflect the development or otherwise of the writer's mental prowess, but conditioned by his emotional factor.

A wide upper loop (see fig. 1) shows a personality which has to

10 months old now and his

fig 1 *m female and I work full time*

I really enjoy reading your

looking forward to getting your

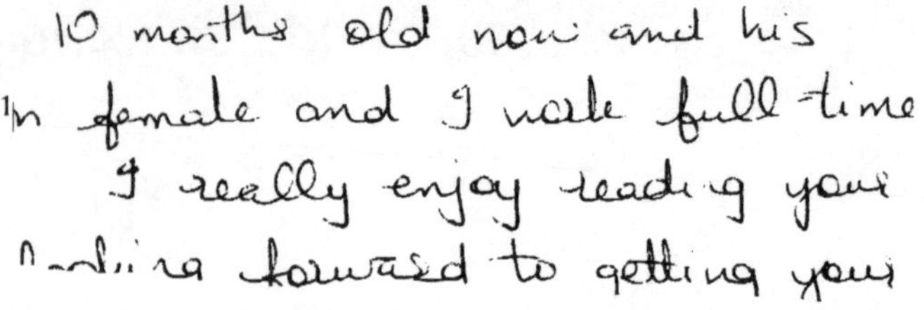

express itself through the writer's emotions and is typical of the entertainer, actor, musician or singer, whether amateur or professional.

Tall loops, those unusually high in proportion to the size of the middle zone (fig. 2), indicate a visionary type of imagination and belongs to someone who delights in the world of fantasy.

fig 2

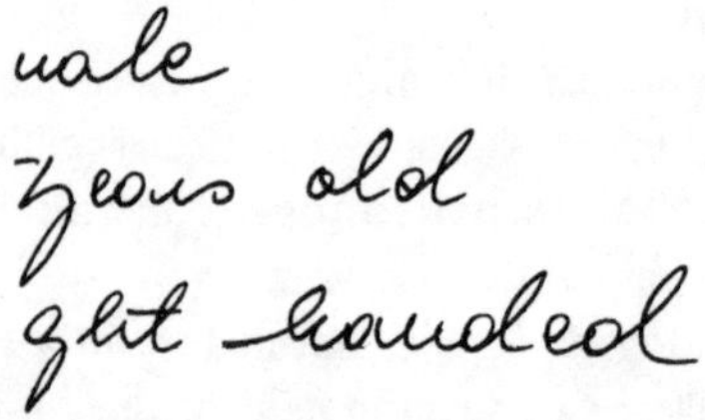

male

years old

left handed

The wide, high loop with a slightly square look to it (see fig. 3) suggests a certain amount of aggression or a rigid, rather stubborn way of dealing with others.

fig 3

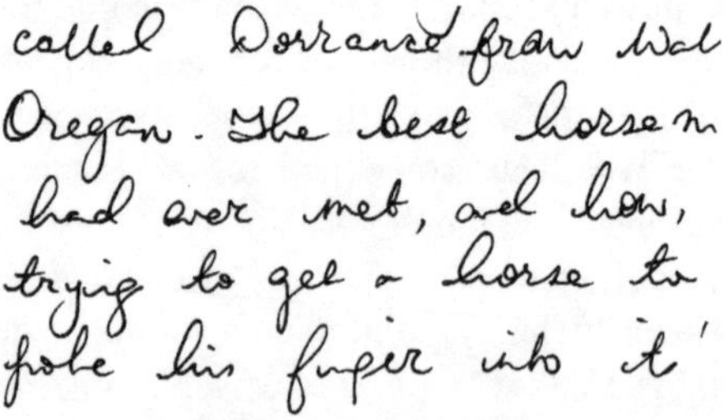

called Dorrance from Wal Oregon. The best horse n had ever met, and how, trying to get a horse to poke his finger into it'

When you see exaggerated upper loops (fig. 4), expect the writer to cede to most things. Unfortunately, this writer tends to bottle his feelings until it all gets too much for him – and he blows!

fig 4

Caper Capos

54

Loops that have been retraced (see fig. 5) imply repression and inhibition. This writer will be unable to express his emotional life properly and will resent any intrusion into his private life, for whatever reason. He often has a rather formal general outlook.

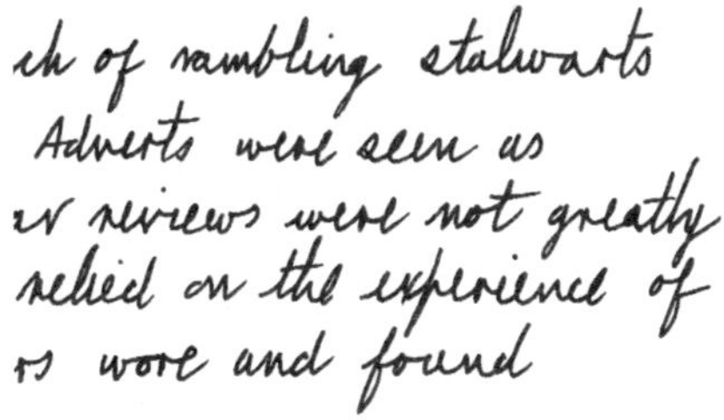

ch of rambling stalwarts
Adverts were seen as
er reviews were not greatly
relied on the experience of
rs wore and found

fig 5

A stroke with what appears to be a balloon-like loop at the top of the letter (see fig. 6) indicates a sense of humour and some originality of thought and ideas. When handwriting is narrow in the middle zone but has this type of loop the writer may be narrowminded.

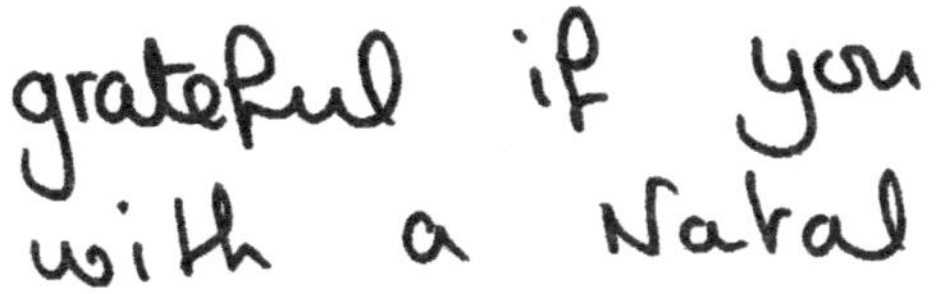

grateful if you
with a Natal

fig 6

If there are pointed tops to a loop (fig. 7) it usually shows the writer to have a level of individuality that extends to rather misplaced ideals that can manifest in a rebel streak. He will deliberately bend or break the rules to suit himself.

I would be grateful to
horoscope. My date & place

fig 7

Narrow loops (see fig. 8) suggest repression and hidden fears. The writer is a dreamer and fantasises. If it comes to putting such ideas into action there will be little or no follow-through.

Many thanks, I look

fig 8

A variety of loops (see fig. 9) shows mixed ideals and a colourful imagination although much will depend on the rest of the script, for a mixture or variety of any feature implies imbalance. The more variety of loops there are the more there will be a disparity of moods.

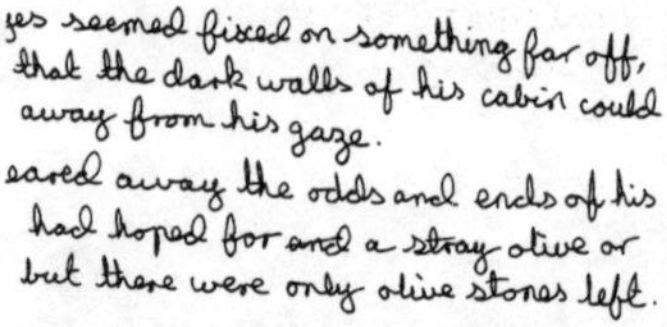

fig 9

yes seemed fixed on something far off,
that the dark walls of his cabin could
away from his gaze.
eased away the odds and ends of his
had hoped for and a stray olive or
but there were only olive stones left.

When loops appear distorted or the shape deviates a lot from the accepted norm (see fig. 10), it indicates an emotionally distorted nature. Look at the construction of the letter and the rest of the writing to detect the probable cause.

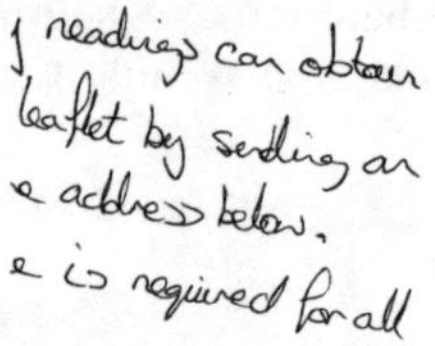

fig 10

readings can obtain
leaflet by sending an
e address below.
e is required for all

A broken upper loop (fig. 11) often appears with the break made more on the upper stroke than on the downstroke. Here, the writer is likely to suffer anxiety problems. He may feel he lacks ability or be uncertain about his feelings, ideals or relationships. Should the break be on the downstroke there may be some physical or mental illness threatening the writer – at the time of writing.

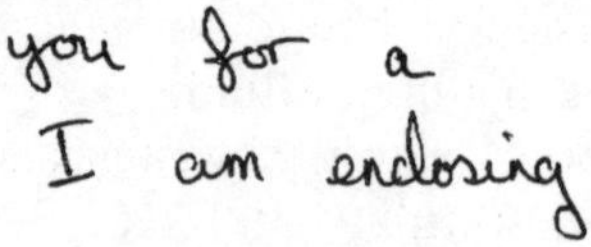

fig 11

you for a
I am enclosing

A stroke or line rather than a loop (see fig. 12) is a sign of repression in the imaginative processes. The writer will have more of a mental approach to emotional matters than a physical one.

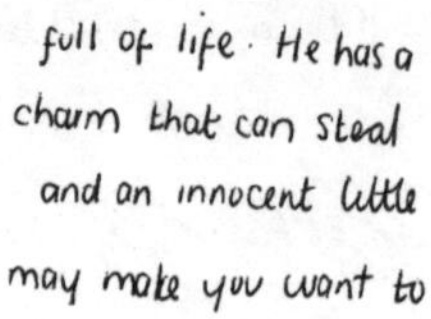

fig 12

full of life. He has a
charm that can steal
and an innocent little
may make you want to

Loops small in proportion to the rest of the script, those that do not reach very high (see fig. 13), implies a rather down-to-earth nature. This type is not overly ambitious and is aware of his limitations. While seen to be reliable, he is not pushy but a down-to-earth and plodding type who might eventually achieve his aims.

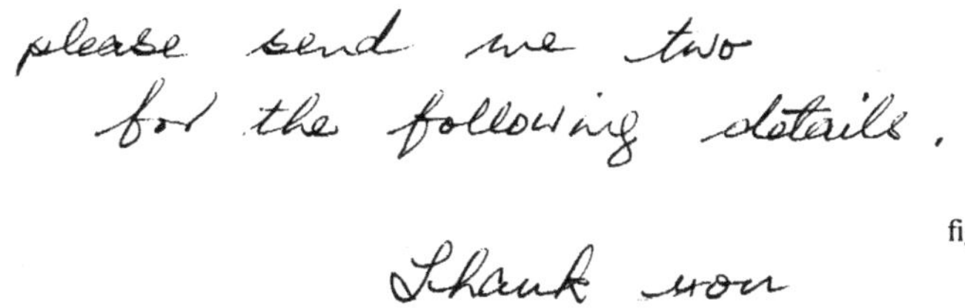

please send me two for the following details.

fig 13

Thank you

When all the loops are in reasonable proportion with the rest of the handwriting and without too much variation (see fig. 14), the writer will have an average, sensible approach to life. Both feet are kept firmly on the ground, and little tends to faze him.

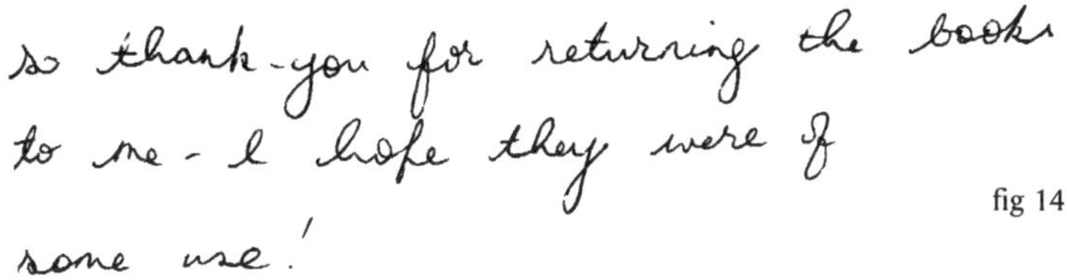

so thank-you for returning the books to me - I hope they were of some use!

fig 14

Lower-zone loops and strokes

In handwriting, the lower zone is concerned with the instinctive and practical side of the nature. More than anywhere, it is here that a writer is likely to betray his natural inclinations. Well-formed lower loops that fit in with the main body of text (see fig. 15) suggest a normal, healthy, well-balanced individual with average drives and instincts.

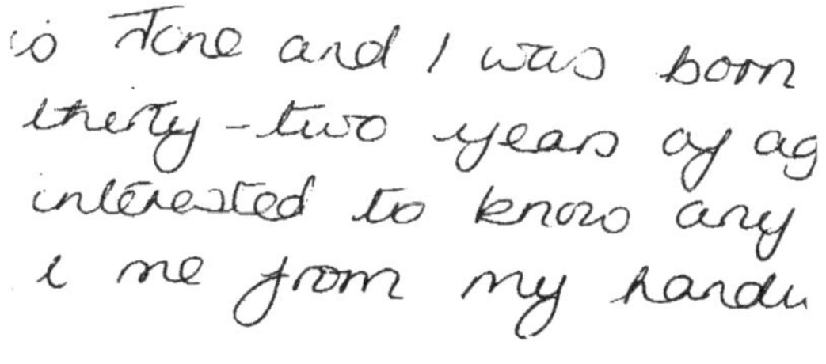

is Tone and I was born thirty-two years of ag interested to know any I me from my hand...

fig 15

A wide lower loop, particularly when triangular in appearance (see fig. 16), is a sign of a contentious nature and attitude. The longer the reach downward, the more this writer will exaggerate, for this is also the mark of a self-opinionated and impulsive character. There is an added tendency to oppose change or innovation, almost as a matter of principle. Basically, this writer is afraid to change and is only confident when on familiar ground.

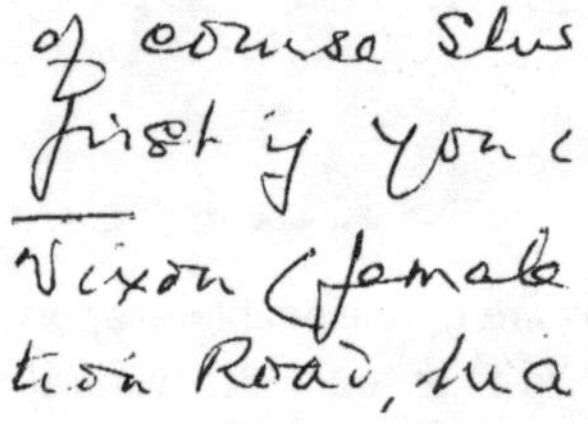

fig 16

A wide, oval-shaped lower loop (fig. 17) denotes a fairly basic character with strong physical drives. This writer sets much store on physical and material matters like achievement, acquisition and possession. There is also a very strong libido.

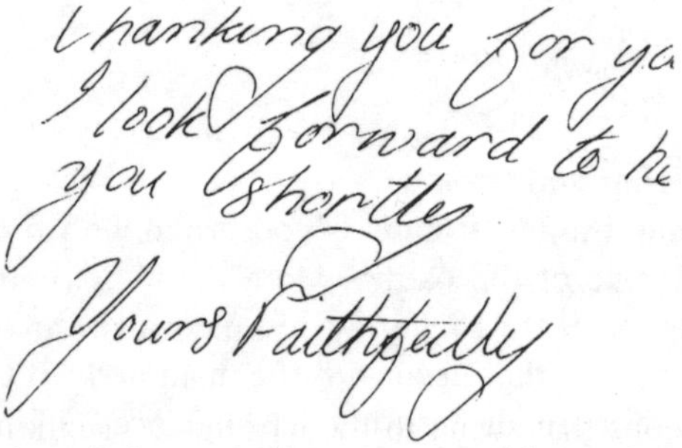

fig 17

Irrespective of size, a broken or ragged lower loop (fig. 18) is linked with a physical health problem. This could reflect a broken or

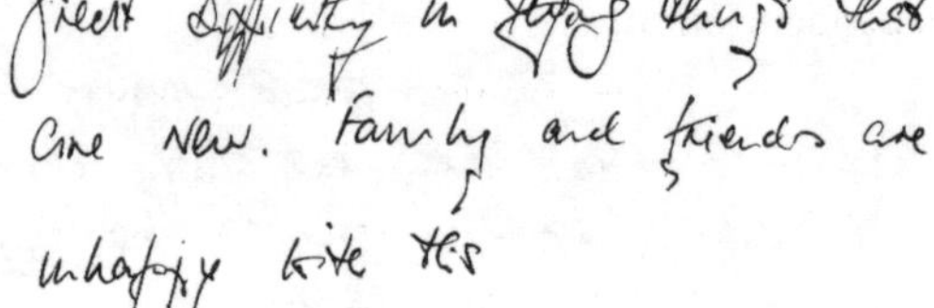

fig 18

deformed lower limb, or it may be a temporary illness involving the loss of the use of a limb.

A small loop that does not reach very far into the lower zone (see fig. 19), is a suggestion of sexual inadequacy or problems in this area. There will also be a lack of stamina and vitality.

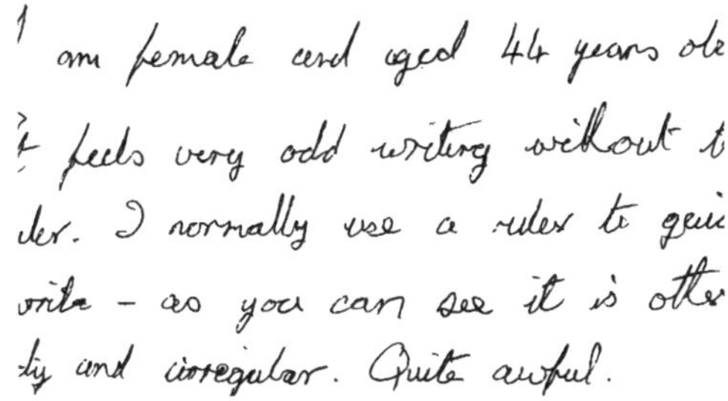

fig 19

Unfinished, open loops that swing wide and to the left (fig. 20) are often found in the writing of impressionable people, especially young, adolescent girls. In older writers it is almost always a sign of an unsatisfactory sex life. The smaller the 'cradle' the more it is likely to reflect unfulfilled sexual expectations.

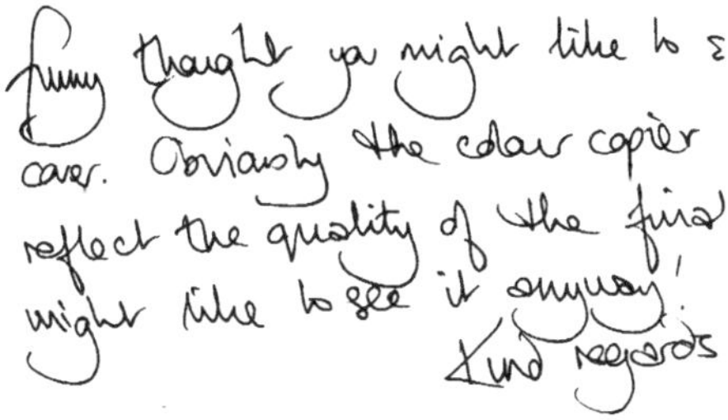

fig 20

Lower loops that swing to the left (fig. 21) suggest difficulty in trying to forget past emotional entanglements. These writers hold on to the past but may have trouble maintaining a sound and reliable relationship with their partners. They are very emotional people and rather dependent on others.

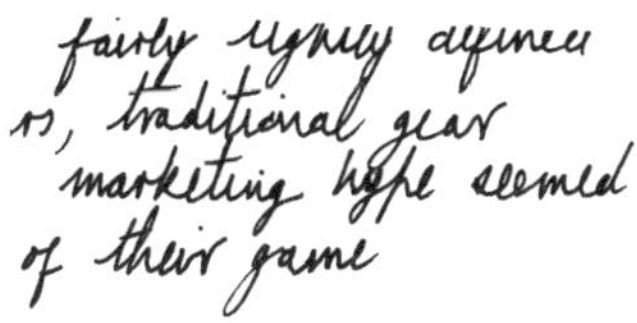

fig 21

59

When lower loops pull to the right (fig. 22) it indicates those who prefer to use their (emotional) energies in more practical ways such as pursuing their ambitions. These emotions, however, are still kept fairly near the surface and are easily stimulated. This writer is usually a very active type.

fig 22

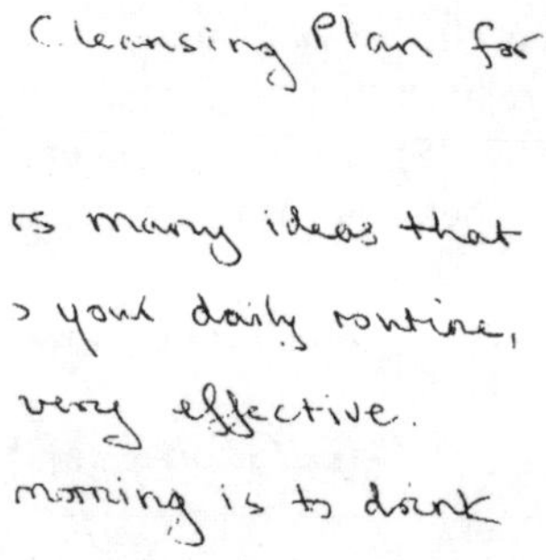

Cleansing Plan for

is many ideas that
> your daily routine,
very effective.
morning is to drink

Claw-like lower loops (see fig. 23) suggests a writer who avoids responsibility or prefers others to make decisions and take the lead. He has the knack of losing himself in a crowd but still keeps his personal aims very much to the fore. He is avaricious, chameleon-like and can be greedy.

fig 23

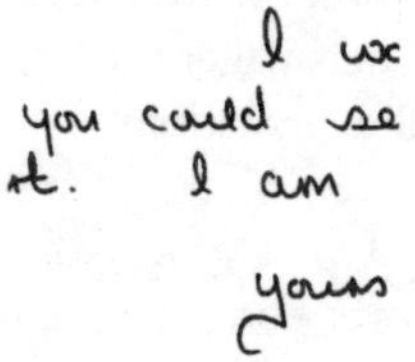

I ux
you could se
t. I am

yours

Loops within loops (fig. 24) show the worrier who, even after all is done and finished, cannot quite bring himself to stop and let go. Such a character can be so doggedly persistent and compulsive that it is embarrassing.

fig 24

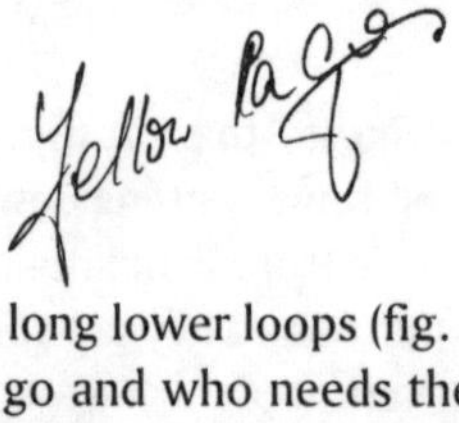

Yellow Pages

Exaggerated or very long lower loops (fig. 25) show restlessness, someone always on the go and who needs the constant stimulation of something new. This type rarely stays on his own for very long for he thrives best in company.

Narrow lower loops (fig. 26) indicate a repressed emotional nature, someone who is unable to physically demonstrate his feelings when he meets or says goodbye to someone close, especially in public.

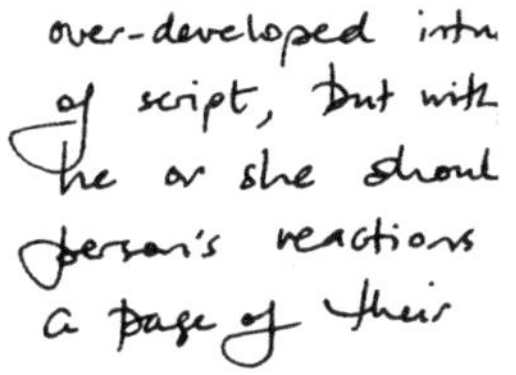

over-developed into
of script, but with
he or she shoul
person's reactions
a page of their

fig 25

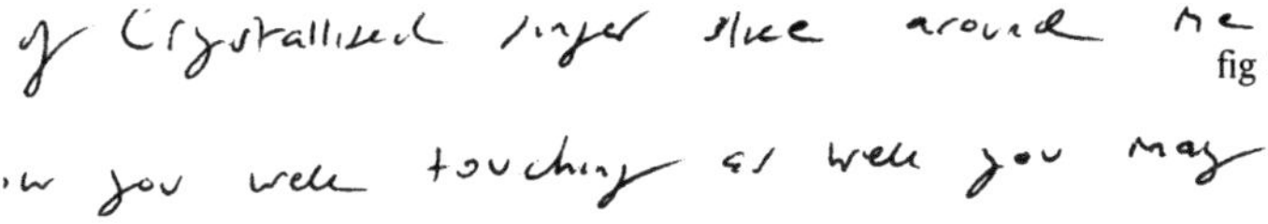

of Crystallised linger slue around the

fig 26

in you well touching as well you may

A retraced stroke rather than a lower loop (fig. 27) shows caution. This writer may be unable to physically express or enjoy love and sex openly. A lot of care and understanding is needed by those whose partners write in such a fashion.

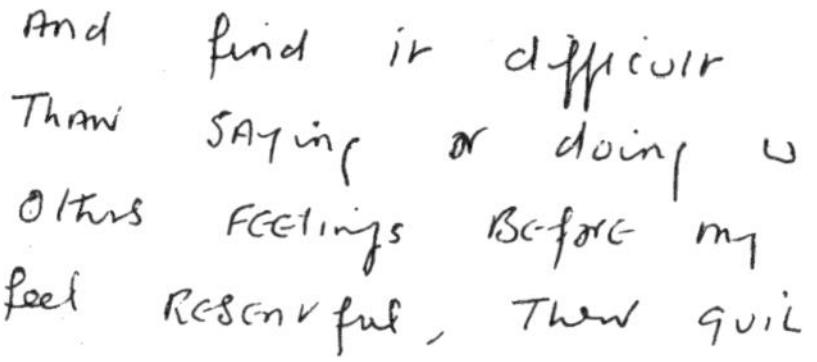

And find it difficult
Than Saying or doing u
Others Feelings Before my
feel Resentful, Then quit

fig 27

A tick at the end of a lower zone stroke (see fig. 28) may move to the left or the right and is a sign of frustration, impatience or both. This writer is not to be toyed with – under any circumstances! If the tick swings to the right of the stroke there will not be so much inner anger as when the tick swings back towards the left.

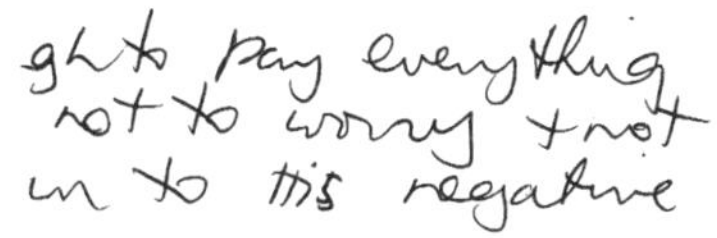

ght to pay everything
not to worry + not
in to this negative

fig 28

A variety of lower loops (see fig. 29 overleaf) shows mixed feelings and attitudes in the writer's basic nature. He will show a markedly changeable outlook and, the more the variety of the loops, the more mood swings will be in evidence.

If, instead of loops a writer makes straight lines as descenders (see fig. 30 overleaf) he may prefer to avoid the physical side of emotional life for as long as he can. This type prefers to experience everything in his mind. The longer the line descends into the lower zone, the more the writer's energy needs to be properly channelled.

fig 29

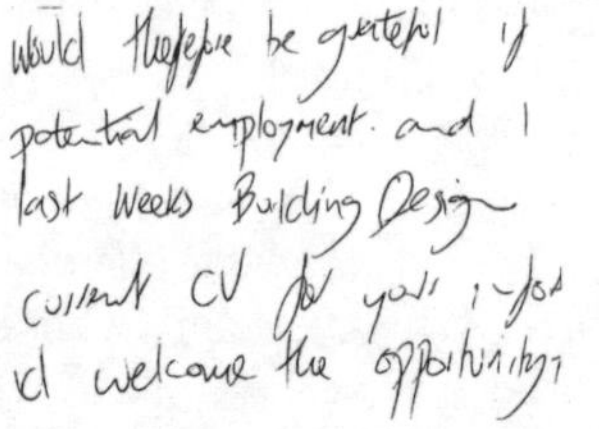

fig 30

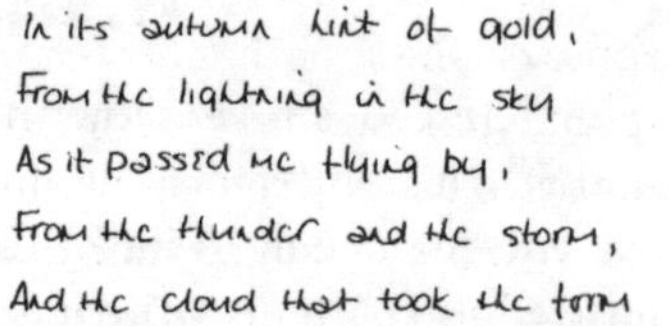

A lower loop made in reverse (fig. 31) indicates a contentious nature. The writer is often a born rebel who will deliberately flout all the conventions. He gets bored very easily, and needs the constant stimulation of change. He will have a slight immature edge to his personality and there will be a keen, if somewhat misplaced sense of humour.

fig 31

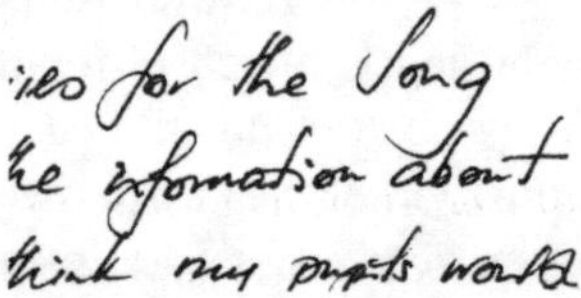

Long, heavy straight lines into the lower zone (fig. 32) shows someone who dislikes opposition. The personality is quite positive and there will be a strong temper. This writer may be thought 'cold' by those around him but this is often just a bluff to avoid too close a relationship.

fig 32

Loops in the middle zone

Strictly speaking, loops should not be seen at all in the middle zone. No letters are formally constructed using a loop. However, there are many occasions when loops are created in the course of handwriting and it is to these intruders we now look.

In English handwriting loops sometimes appear in middle zone oval letters like the a and o, and they are also be seen in the middle zone section of letters like the d, g, p and y. In fact, intruder loops can be seen just about anywhere. Wherever and whenever it appears, the loop implies emotion. If it is seen in places where it should not normally occur, then the writer will be emotionally sensitive and his self-expression may be impaired in some way.

Within the letters a and o may be seen a small loop either to the top left, top right or on both sides at the same time. When loops are seen on the top left of an oval and the oval is also closed (see fig. 33), the writer will be the soul of discretion and have good personal integrity. He can keep a secret.

fig 33

If the loop is on the right-hand side of the oval (fig. 34), the writer is open, friendly but not always too careful about what he says, or to whom. He means no harm, he just doesn't think.

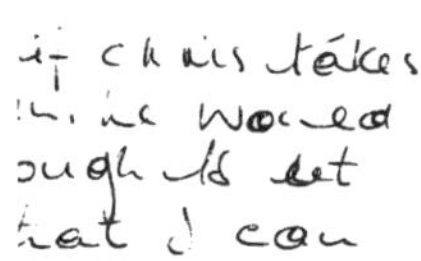

fig 34

If double loops are seen (fig. 35 overleaf), the writer deceives himself and others, but not necessarily in any dishonest way. He simply is not always as honest with himself as he should be. He may not recognize his limitations by promising too much, or fail to agree to do something because he feels he cannot do it. Personal discipline is rather poor.

fig 35

Dear Sir,

Please can you

A loop instead of a single stroke is sometimes seen to form the stem of the letter d from its base in the middle zone (see fig. 36). Here, the writer shows that he is sensitive to criticism and worries a bit too much about what others may think. The bigger the loop the more this is so. Should the loop seem to have a squarish top to it, he will also be obstinate and aggressive.

fig 36

would you send me

When a loop forms the stem of the letter t (see fig. 37), the writer will lack confidence. He will do quite well so long as he receives constant praise and approbation. A 'please' and a 'thank-you' work wonders here; this writer has to be asked and not told to do things. The wider the loop the more talkative and sensitive the nature.

fig 37

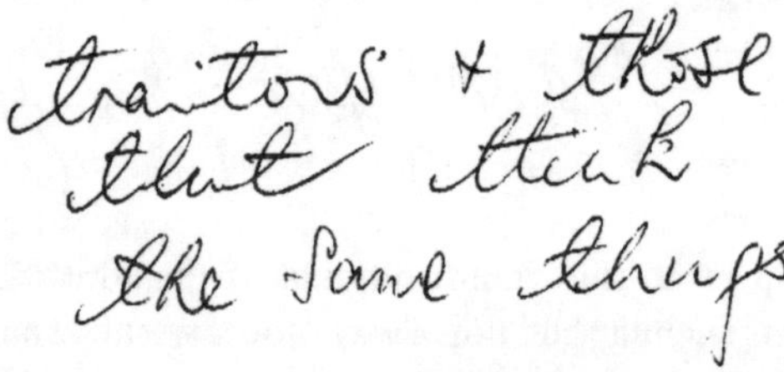

traitors + those that think the same things

When loops are formed in places where they would not normally be seen then an implication of emotional sensitivity will be present in the writer's nature. Whether this is defensive or aggressive may be inferred from the rest of the script.

7

Capital Letters, First and Last Strokes

Making an entrance

When an actor makes his appearance on a stage he does so in one of several ways. The moment may call for a high profile, dashing or flamboyant entrance; it might need the actor to simply sidle on; or it may need a plain and simple walk-on. An entertainer who is about to appear on a television talk-show makes his entrance according to his mood or, more to the point perhaps, that which is expected of him by his adoring public: the entrance that he feels will adequately serve the situation. And so it is with the way we write our capital letters for they are the equivalent of our entrance, our introduction to other people. How we do this is very important in some circumstances but less so in others.

Capital letters signify the amount of self-confidence the writer has in himself and his abilities. One look at the way a writer's capital letters compares with the rest of his script says a lot about him. Indeed, when writing for a job interview or promotion this takes on an added importance. If the letter is to a friend it shows how he values that relationship. Then there is the very private love letter, to be read only by the writer and his loved one, that can speak absolute volumes about that association.

Remember, a capital letter initiates things, like the actor as he makes his entrance. Think about this when you assess how the writer makes an impact on you right from the first letter of the first word. Do not forget either to look at where and how the writer places his address on the paper. Look at the start of individual sentences and paragraphs for consistency or otherwise.

The average handwriting size is about nine mm overall or three mm for each of the zones. Few people write that precisely, so when there is any marked divergence in size it will be quite obvious. When there is little obvious difference, then the balance between the zones is quite even (see fig. 1) suggesting the writer has a well-balanced inner nature and is reasonably objective in his overall outlook. He will show a matter-of-fact, efficient and no-nonsense approach to problems.

fig 1 *Nature is not mute.*

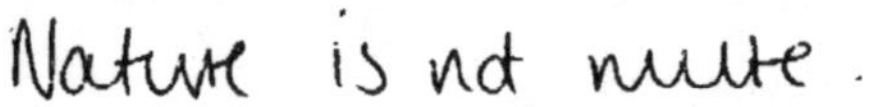

On average, a slight variation of size as the letter progresses is to be expected and merely reflects a competent, quiet, mature type who can handle just about anything that comes his way.

However, if the capital letters are much larger than the rest of the script (see fig. 2) the writer needs to be recognized, and sets great store by status and position. He is proud and ambitious and will exhibit a certain amount of ostentation.

fig 2 *Dear Sandra,*

Many
Thanks

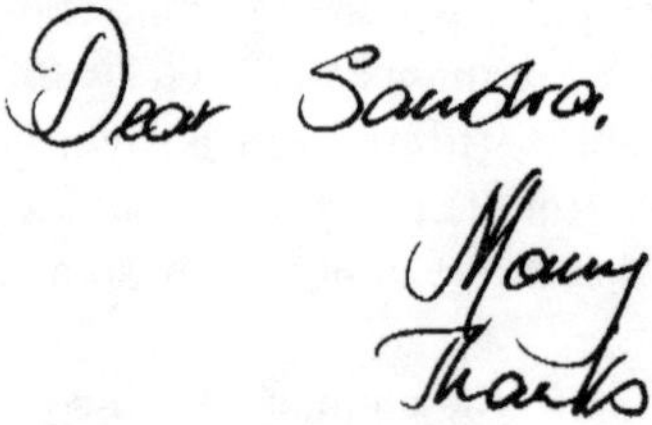

Small capital letters (see fig. 3) suggest a lack of confidence. The writer lacks push and drive and has little vitality. He is unassuming, quite modest and may prefer to work or play in the background. The nature will also be slightly reserved, but sympathetic to the problems of other people. This writer provides a good shoulder to cry on.

fig 3 *I'm sure there are*
Astrology - I find it t
At present I am try
s gives meaning to

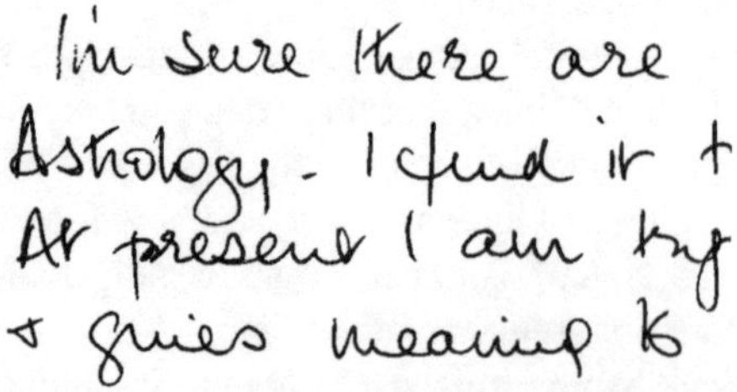

Broad, wide capital letters (fig. 4) symbolize the show-off. This writer is likely to be extravagant and wasteful, inclined to arrogance and overly ambitious. He can exhibit poor taste, often without his realizing. If there is any unusual ornamentation he will be crude as well. This writer can do no wrong – in his eyes.

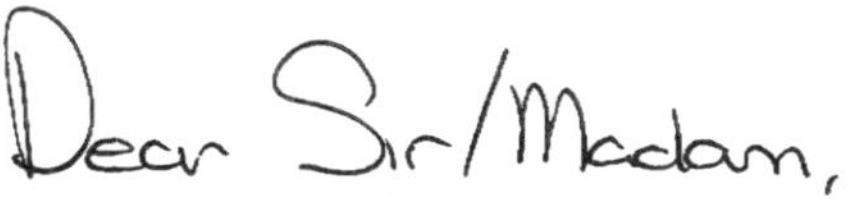

fig 4

Ornate capitals (fig. 5) suggest a pompous, fussy, vulgar type who may try to bluff his way through situations and life in general. He is likely to have a gambling streak.

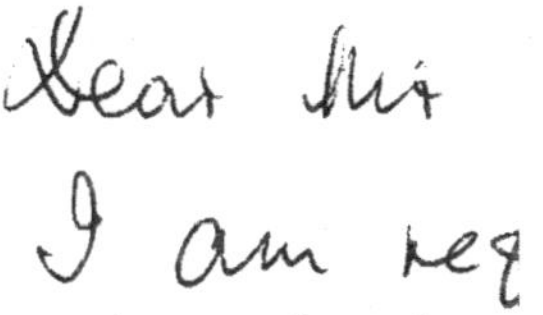

fig 5

A capital letter that stands away from the rest of the word (see fig. 6) shows a writer prepared to listen to his intuition or play hunches. The character may be known for his 'lucky' guesses when it comes to minor matters of chance.

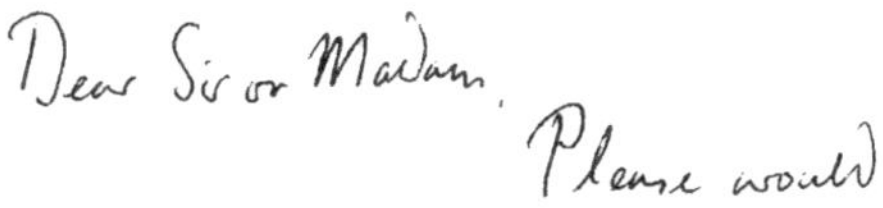

fig 6

A capital letter joined to the rest of the word (fig. 7) implies fluency of thought. There is very little allowance for chance. He will work out just about everything well in advance to minimize the possibility of errors.

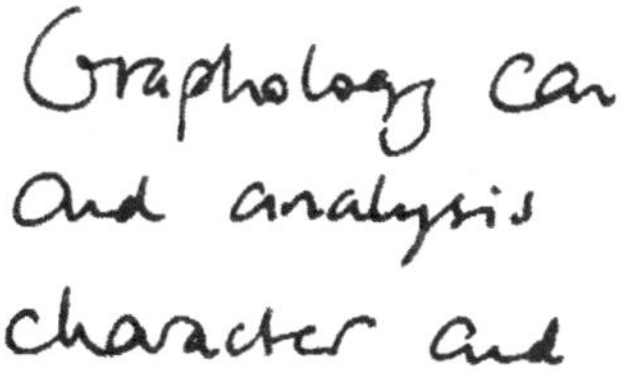

fig 7

Humour is shown by those little extras added by the writer which obviously do not belong (see fig. 8 overleaf). This suggests a co-operative, friendly and open type. Look at the colour of the ink – it might show if this is a contrived or a natural gesture.

fig 8

Occasionally, capital letters appear in the wrong place such as the middle of a sentence or word (see fig. 9). The writer was unsettled at the time of writing, but frequent misplaced capitals are nearly always a sign of deception: the writer may be lying.

fig 9

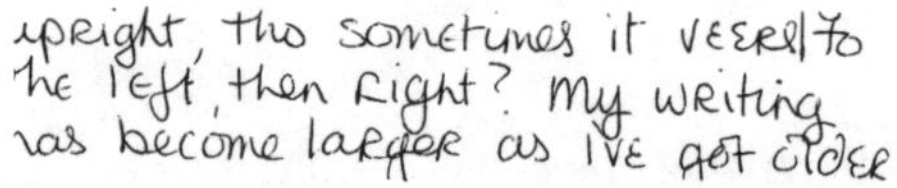

upright, tho sometimes it veers to the left, then right? My writing has become larger as I've got older

Lead-in strokes

Let us return to the analogy of the actor and the way he makes an entrance. The moment may call for him to have a prop – a hat or a cane perhaps. He may have to produce something after he has made his entrance or, and this is very important, he might be called on to produce or throw something on *before* he enters. This is a very important moment, and unless properly performed, it can make or mar a performance. So it is with handwriting and, in particular, with the capital or initial letter. If the first letter of a word or a sentence is made with any embellishment or extra strokes, this is important.

Long starting strokes suggest inner doubt. The writer dislikes to make mistakes or, more to the point, be seen to make mistakes. He prefers to do things by the book and often allows others to lead. He may well dislike change, and worries about how he appears to others.

Lead-in strokes from the base-line or below it (see fig. 10) suggest problems from the past that can still give rise to emotional tension or even anxiety. This really is a prop for the writer, almost like a child's security blanket.

Lead-in strokes from the upper zone (fig. 11) means the writer will always have to show off his intelligence. This one loves to boast and prove he is clever. He is not always likeable.

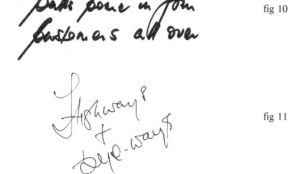

fig 10

fig 11

An arcade-style lead-in stroke (see fig. 12) suggests that the writer has some element of secrecy in his nature. He might have something to hide, or may not be entirely honest with himself or even with those who are very close to him.

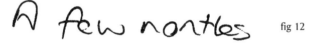

fig 12

Angular lead-in strokes (fig. 13) indicate the writer who is resentful of past losses, self-inflicted or not. The nature is inclined to be critical, reserved, suspicious or plain downright self-defensive, especially if or when challenged for any reason.

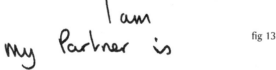

fig 13

Garland lead-in strokes (fig. 14 overleaf) suggest a warm and friendly nature. The writer is sentimental, has a lazy streak and is easily moved in any appeal to his emotions. He does not like to be alone for too long and needs to be with people to bring out the best in him.

Thread-like lead-in strokes (fig. 15 overleaf) show someone who cannot or will not make decisions because of uncertainty and a lot of built-in self-doubt. This is the sign of a follower not a leader.

fig 14

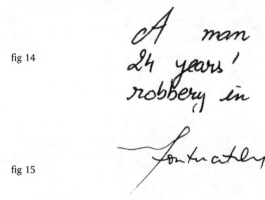

fig 15

If the lead-in stroke is long the writer will exhibit much drama in the way he carries on. He loves attention, is flirtatious and not always honest. He tends to bend the truth to suit the moment, but not necessarily for any dishonest purpose.

When there are hooks or ticks on, or as, lead-in strokes (see fig. 16) then the writer will be irritable, even irascible in some cases, and not easy to approach. He will possess a carping, critical nature, not only of other people and/or the 'system', but also of himself. He will set great store by acquisition and possession.

fig 16

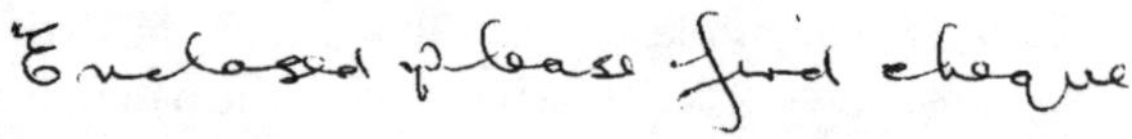

Final strokes

As the actor leaves the stage after a performance he will do so in many ways. It is possible that his way of saying goodbye may have a similar quality to his entrance, or it may possibly be a totally different matter entirely. Whatever he does, he will be known for it. Of course, the role he plays has a lot to do with it, but his exit will have his special mark.

It is the same with the final strokes of letters, sentences or paragraphs. Of course, the proper final stroke is contained in the writer's signature and is dealt with in that chapter. The final stroke provides clues to the writer's social attitude, the way he views the future, his mood and general disposition at the time of writing. These strokes also allow us to detect speed in handwriting.

Speed implies spontaneity and suggests objective thinking. It is a reflection of the writer's natural behaviour. Any error made because of the speed of thought, or the inability of the hand to keep up with the mind shows the level of co-ordination between the hand and the mind.

This is a good starting point for the investigation of forgery. No impulse is so difficult to control as when it must be stopped, only to be allowed free rein again, for this is what happens when we write in a normal manner. We finish one word, stop and lift the pen very slightly, put the pen back to the paper and then begin the next word or sentence. This is a most difficult act to copy with any degree of accuracy.

A fast writer is not comfortable writing slowly, nor is a slow writer when he tries to hurry. Thus, social adaptability, habit and mood can all be detected from the way in which a last letter has been constructed.

The absence of an ending stroke (fig. 17) shows someone who may not always observe social niceties. Such writers do not look for or need the approval of others. They are direct, self-controlled and careful. They are known to mistrust the motives of others and often appear to be quite rude by those who do not know them.

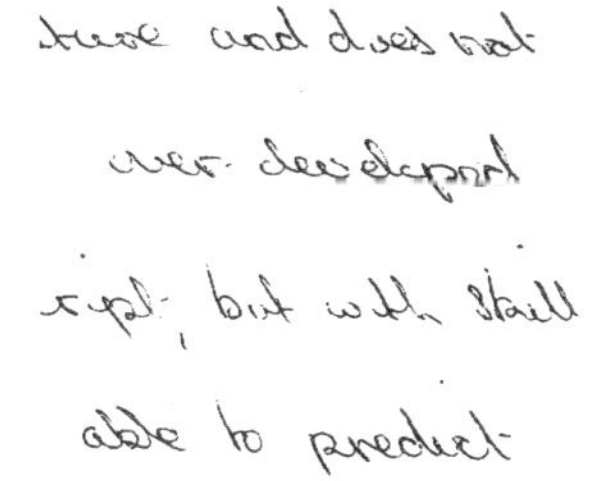

fig 17

A final stroke that swings outwards and upwards (fig. 18) shows activity, drive and enthusiasm. If the stroke is over-long the implication is one of tenacity.

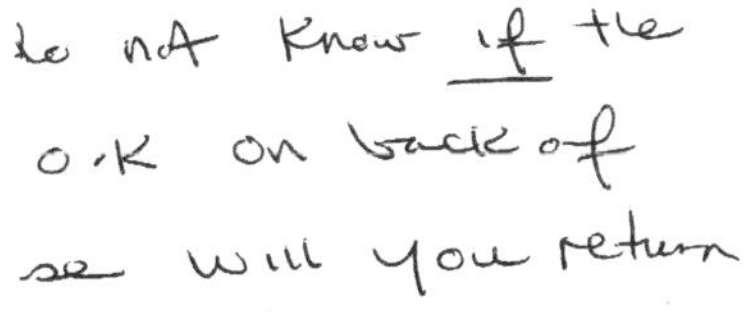

fig 18

fig 19

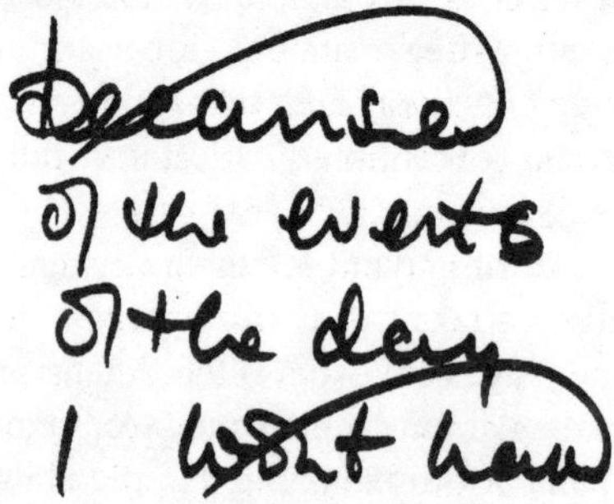

A defensive and self protective attitude prevails when the end stroke curves up and over the last letter (see fig. 19); this will be taken to an extreme if the whole word is covered. The writer may do almost anything to keep himself out of trouble, real or imagined, and is likely to deliberately deceive to achieve this.

If the endstroke returns back through the last word (fig. 20) it is an indication of an introverted and untrusting nature. This writer is rather negative and may have some self-destructive tendencies.

fig 20

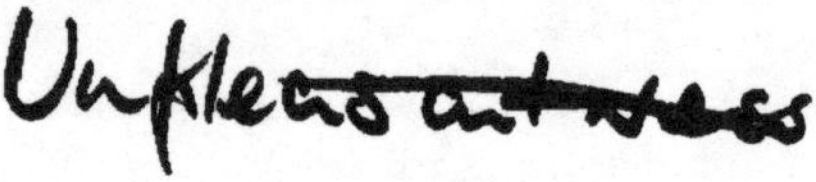

Final strokes that descend below the base-line (fig. 21) show intolerance and an unfriendly nature. This writer will exhibit aggression, obstinacy and prejudice. He also has to have the last word.

fig 21

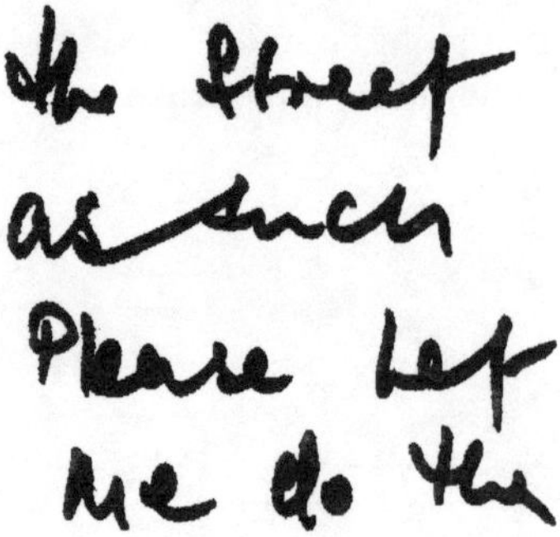

When a final letter is incomplete or not finished properly the writer will have a brusque manner with scant regard for social niceties. When there are hooks and ticks on final strokes he is liable to be argumentative, contentious, critical and not always satisfied with his lot. He is equally markedly possessive.

An ending stroke of garland appearance suggests a responsive and open nature and a talker. The arcade type is less outgoing and more secretive and may seem ever on the defensive.

An angular ending stroke implies a more disciplined personality but not without some aggression. The thready endstroke suggests a lack of attention to detail. However, the writer usually manages to complete most tasks – his way. Occasionally, endstrokes may swing downwards and under the last letter or the whole word. This shows materialism and selfishness. The writer may be unable to mix well in company. Initially, this type appears polished and confident on the surface but inwardly, they are often lonely and uncertain.

If there are hooks on the endstrokes the writer will need very careful handling. If the hooks turn downwards, the writer will be materialistic and rather stubborn. If the hooks turn upwards, he will be acquisitive, full of his own importance but rather conventional – although this may be a front.

When the majority of endstrokes go straight down it suggests a certain amount of intolerance, with strong likes and dislikes.

Endstrokes made horizontally mean anything from extravagance to generosity depending on the rest of the script.

8

Envelope Addressing

The way a writer addresses an envelope reveals quite a lot about his personal esteem and general ego. Not many people pay much attention to the way they prepare their envelope, but a good few do try to make sure it is at least legible – if only to ensure safe delivery! We receive our first impression of a writer from the way he has written the address and where he has positioned it. An envelope has not only to be written legibly, but the address should also be placed according to convention: most writers are well aware of this. In fact, from time to time the Post Office runs an advertising promotion to ensure some convention is followed, for computers are now used to sort mail.

Therefore, how an envelope is written must be considered as the outward expression of a writer's attitude towards other people; it is also where a selection of capital letters and numbers may be found all in one place.

Writing on an envelope can often differ from the way the letter inside has been written. As a rule, the writing is slightly larger in size, for it is here that many people intensify their personal ego to try to impress the addressee. When the writing on the envelope is smaller than that contained in the main body of the letter it should be seen as a suggestion of false modesty. The size of the writing in the letter will confirm this. However, many writers fail to hide their true nature when they address an envelope. Thus, a smaller script here can show they are not as confident as they may imply when these two writings are compared.

Writing on an envelope more or less the same size as the writing inside reveals a well-balanced nature, someone who behaves in a fairly constant way whether they are in public or in private.

When the writing on the envelope is virtually illegible the writer may have a difficult social life. He does not always observe the usual niceties, can be contentious, cares very little for others and, if not tactless, is certainly thoughtless and rude. Illegible handwriting on an envelope, if nothing else, is plain bad manners. Many overlook this small but very important point. It is a matter of simple courtesy and many people are genuinely unaware they lack this.

The actual placing of an address on the envelope says a lot about a writer. Convention requires the address should be placed as centrally as possible, but this does not happen very often. When it does the writer shows good balance and judgment.

Before we proceed any further, and to help analyse the way the address is placed on the envelope, fold it once lengthwise and once the other way so that when you reopen it you will find you have created four equal divisions (fig. 1).

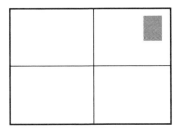

fig 1

The top half represents future matters, ambitions, aspirations and hopes. The bottom half shows how we normally relate to material things, possessions, instincts and drives.

The left-hand side of the envelope equates with matters of the past, our ego and memories while the right-hand side shows how we view the future, our initiative and how active we are.

When an address occupies the top half of the envelope (fig. 2) the writer will be a bit of a dreamer and something of an idealist. He may also lack confidence and objectivity. There may not be a lot of respect for the addressee.

fig 2

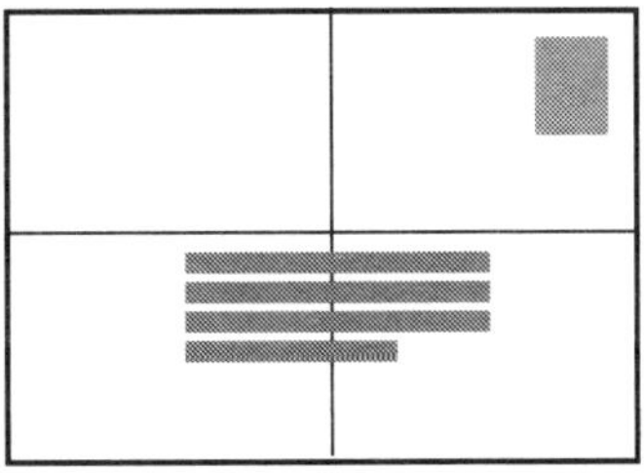

fig 3

If the address is written more to the bottom of the envelope (fig. 3) the writer will be a materialist, impulsive and rather pessimistic. He will also be practical, possessive and could be a collector.

When the address is placed more towards the top left-hand side of the envelope (fig. 4) it indicates an enquiring mind, but there may also be some timidity or a lack of self-confidence; this writer will be reserved or exhibit caution in his ways.

When the address is written more towards the top right-hand side of the envelope (fig. 5) the writer is careless and does not have very good planning ability. He has obviously forgotten that the stamp should go in this corner. It could be a lack of respect for the usual conventions or just plain forgetfulness.

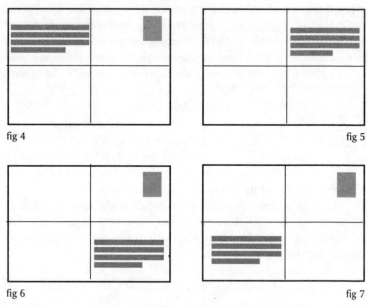

fig 4

fig 5

fig 6

fig 7

When the address is placed more towards the bottom right-hand side of the envelope (fig. 6), the writer is straightforward, independent up to a point and practical.

If the address is placed at the bottom left-hand side of the envelope (fig. 7) the writer is materialistic, little gets past him, and what does is of little use to anyone else. There is an over-cautious or general air of reserve in the make-up.

The stepped address, from the top left to the bottom right of an envelope (fig. 8) is a mark of respect and the conventional way. This is traditional, as taught in school, and comes naturally with us into adulthood. This writer is cautious with those he does not know very well and does not like to be hurried into making decisions.

In some countries it is an accepted practice to underline parts of the address: the street, town or county, perhaps (fig. 9). This can be done with or without a ruler or by using a different coloured ink. Some take this to extremes and emphasize everything, which is a pointless exercise. By doing this, the writer defeats the object of the emphasis – obviously someone who is unable to distinguish between the important and the unimportant. Such a writer is often awkward, obstinate, stubborn and unable to see very far ahead, and is unable to let go of a situation long after the matter has been resolved. This smacks of compulsion, and when this underlining is also found in the body of the letter the writer might need treatment.

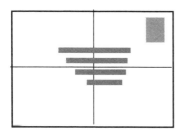

fig 8

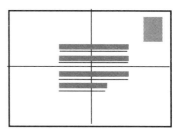

fig 9

These guidelines are, of course, conditioned by the handwriting style: slant, slope, and connections, pressure and size.

It is widely thought there has to be some form of control in the way an envelope is addressed and that it is not as spontaneously written as the main body of the letter. This is not always the case, for many people dash off the envelope without thinking. So take the time to examine an envelope. Whatever the differences may be, strong or slight, they are very revealing.

9

Left-handedness

There are no hard and fast reasons why some people are left-handed or others are right-handed. The left-hand side of the brain controls the right side of the body, and that includes the right hand. Whether a person writes with their right or left hand, the right hand is normally acknowledged to be the dominant. The left side of the brain, the master hemisphere, is much more developed than the right, whether the subject is a left-hander or not.

The left-hand side of the brain is responsible for judgment and intelligence and two important features of cognition, reading and writing, are located in the left hemisphere of right-handers. In left-handed subjects this is reversed.

One should not associate left-handedness with poor perception or intelligence because, generally speaking, the majority of left-handers are bright and perceptive. They have learned to exist in the more predominant right-handed world and, in general, this does tend to make them more perceptive than average. There are not many poorly educated or 'slow' left-handed people.

Generally speaking, people tend to favour one hand over the other for most activities, but very few are truly ambidextrous. While we may use both hands with an equal facility, we do find it easier to be selective and are far better carrying out some activities with one hand than with the other. Of course, there will be a difference in the skills we show for certain activities depending on the hand we use and, as a result, there will be a slight preference to use one hand over the other for particular tasks.

Most ambidextrous people prefer to write or draw holding the pen with either their left or their right hand: very few people use both hands with equal facility. In sport, if throwing a ball for example, a normally right-handed person may find the left hand more comfortable to use. Some who are naturally right-handed tend to use their left hand when they have to hold a bat or a racquet.

As a rule, those who are basically right-handed find it difficult or even awkward to use their left hand even for a few moments. If you are normally right-handed try to use a pair of scissors for a few moments. Hold your toothbrush with your left hand, or try to use a knife and fork using opposite hands. It feels strange, because the control you have over this day-to-day piece of equipment seems poor. However, when you use a spoon there are fewer problems. Many folk can and do use a spoon with either hand with equal facility, often without realizing that they do it. Try to sweep, unscrew the top of a jar, strike a match, deal cards or comb your hair with your 'wrong' hand. It is a most unusual feeling.

Just over one hundred years ago some six per cent of the population in the United Kingdom were estimated to be left-handed. From one of the most recently conducted surveys it is now thought there are some nine million left-handers in the country. (1995: 14–15 per cent). Recent American surveys differ slightly from state to state but they put the rate at about 18–20 per cent of the population and different countries have different figures.

In the UK we assume our children will be right-handed unless we are proved wrong by the child. Once a youngster reaches out and picks up objects with his left hand most parents will offer the opportunity to use the right hand or actually place the item in the right hand. Less than fifty years ago we would have normally prevented a left-handed superiority taking hold in a child; today we do not think very much of it. Also, while parents respond accordingly they should never try to force a child to use the hand which they do not naturally select. If an infant appears slower to learn a particular activity it is much better to let his natural instincts have free rein than to try to influence him one way or another.

When assessing handwriting for left-handedness you should do so under a very strong magnifying glass. The 'grain' of the stroke will be made in reverse, from the right to the left rather than the normal left to right. I-dots, especially when made with a 'dash' stroke, and the t-bar crossings are made in this way in the left-handed person's handwriting.

Most right-handers hold writing instruments in much the same way as everyone else, but left-handers employ one of only two styles.

They may write by curling their left arm round so the hand is above the writing but with the pen and hand tilted slightly back toward the body. This is universally known as the 'hook': the writer pulls the pen over the paper and is the most common pen-hold that left-handers tend to use. The alternative method that left-handers use is when they push the pen across the page.

Left Hand Grip

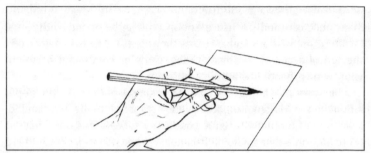

Right Hand Grip

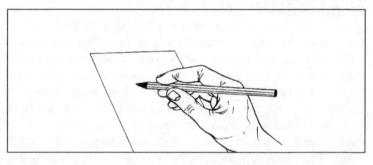

But whatever style a writer uses, in most cases any handwriting problems that he is likely to meet are made considerably easier if he holds the pen slightly higher up the barrel than normal. Simply raising the hold a few centimetres up the barrel will help achieve an easier and far better controlled path over the paper. Such simple remedial action also helps prevent the smudging of the written work – a reward in itself. This action gives far better control of the pen, and the writer is able to see what he writes. It also allows the writer a much better concentration rate as well.

For a graphologist to know whether the writer is left-handed or right-handed is important because it gives him an accurate indication of how the writer is liable to react or behave in emergencies or moments of stress.

Many left-handed writers tend to find a backward slope easier to maintain, and it is a far more natural action for them. Backward, or the left-handed slant implies a sense of introversion when made by a right-handed writer. The writing of a left-handed person, however, does not have the same interpretation. People who write with their left hand are just naturally following the easiest way to perform the act. It is essential that the graphologist is made aware of this from the start and is one of the reasons why graphologists ask about handedness prior to making their analyses.

I have said elsewhere that left-handed people have had to learn to adapt in a basically right-handed society. They are often, and rightfully in my opinion, to be regarded as more alert, intelligent and perceptive than their right-handed counterparts. Never underestimate them.

10
Ink and Paper Colours

All of us are affected in some way by colour. It plays a far more important role in our lives than we may at first appreciate. For many, what we want to wear depends very much on the prevailing mood of the moment. We all have our own personal inclinations when it comes to decorating our homes: what we want for the bedroom, bathroom, sitting-room or kitchen. And what we choose reflects our personal tastes.

When colour is used constructively, that is, the right colour in the right place and not out of context with our surroundings, it can be a most useful aid to successful living.

Colour is associated with mood and behavioural patterns, and our responses to them are extremely revealing. We often speak of black or blue moods, or associate yellow with religious matters or cowardice. We refer to being red with rage, white with temper or green with envy. Brown suggests caution. We know the ancients were aware of the power of colour healing.

In recent times we have re-discovered some of this knowledge and used it in a number of ways. One way has been to decorate public places in certain colours to influence people's behaviour. Green and yellow, for example, are now to be found in airport corridors and lounges for they are thought to have a calming effect. Blue also has a calming effect, but in a different way to green and yellow, while red is quite stimulating. Green represents nature in all its glory while yellow reminds us of the sun and its life-giving powers.

We all have our own personal and favourite colours. According to pyschologists what we choose tends to reflect the nature of our personality.

Red suggests an impulsive nature, excitable and active, someone who likes to be in the forefront of everything.

Blue implies a laid-back, easy-going type who will not be rushed into anything. There may even be an indulged lazy streak.

Green indicates a cautious type. He does not trust too easily in people and things and likes time to himself.

Yellow inclines people to an active life and suggests someone who is perceptive, intelligent and copes well with most things – even surprises.

Brown shows someone fond of the best things in life, food, drink, good company and life's little luxuries.

Those who prefer purple are impressed with the top drawer of just about everything, are ambitious, often snobbish and arrogant.

Grey reflects the loner, one who maintains a very good personal control, is self-sufficient, but can seem cold by nature.

These very brief pen pictures are a reasonable insight of what to expect of a writer when it comes to the colour of ink he chooses to write with in normal circumstances. And to a slightly lesser degree, the colour of the paper he prefers also has a bearing. It is important to remember that this must be the colour a writer consistently employs from personal choice, and not just the pen or paper he has picked up to dash off a note.

The vast majority of writers use blue ink, probably because it is most readily available. The main preference is light blue and is associated with an out-going, sympathetic type who is normally straightforward, loyal to friends and employers. Pale blue tends to be used more by women with creative or artistic inclinations, especially those who like to be noticed.

Royal blue is used more by those who choose positions where they may be responsible for others in some way. Dark blue ink is used as a matter of course in many occupations. It is traditionally assumed to be used by editors, from where we get the term 'blue pencil'. Experience shows they prefer red.

Red is used by those who have to be noticed. There is a love of being different, of excitement and energy. However, the emotional nature of this writer can be easily disturbed for they are very much subject to their emotions. They must experience everything at first hand for themselves.

Green ink implies a disturbed or immature emotional outlook. This writer cannot stand being just one of a crowd. He will be a show-off who likes the limelight and is very individualistic. Often, this writer will use the circle i-dot in his writing.

Those who habitually use brown ink like to be noticed but can be afraid to make any move without first ensuring adequate security, for these people always have safety in mind. They dislike taking a chance or gambling.

Violet ink implies emotional immaturity, whatever the age. They are social butterflies – especially the women. They always have good personal charm, elegance, grace and a delicacy of approach. The men may be slightly effeminate, weak-willed and submissive. For either sex, the past holds more for them than the future.

Theatrical presentations of white, silver, grey, yellow or gold writing on any paper of any colour show an impractical approach, unless, of course, the missive is a kind of invitation. However, the writer who consistently uses yellow or gold ink on a regular basis may be very intuitive. The consistent use of grey or silver ink signifies a need for independence.

Black ink is used by those who must be clearly understood at all times. Status means much; this writer nearly always has a driving ambition. There is a need to achieve, to get to the top. These writers often seem cold and calculating at times and there is often more than just a hint of intolerance. It does not take these writers long to get to the top and, once there, stay there.

These guidelines only relate to the habitual, preferred choice of coloured ink. Nothing can be inferred if the writer has picked up a pen with coloured ink because nothing else was available at the time. People can and do experiment with colours and fashions as they pass through phases, particularly when they are growing up. But despite this, whatever their choice of colour, it is a free one, and so reflects their behavioural patterns.

The choice of stationery and its colour is also free, except when others make gifts in shades most of us would prefer not to use. Permutations of paper colour can now be legion. If at all possible, try to find out the colour the writer normally uses before making an assessment.

Occasionally, one might see a sample of writing where the initial letter of each sentence or paragraph is written in a different colour ink to that of the main body of text. For example, all the initial letters may be written in red ink but the rest of the letter is all in blue or black ink, something also seen in typewritten material. This writer is obsessive and over-fussy. It is unwise to be too critical of him no matter how much he insists that you should be open and honest. He will not take kindly to any criticism, no matter how well meant it may be. He is likely to be unpredictable and suffer from hypochondria, but this should not be taken as a definite sign on its own. This writer can also be extraordinarily diet-conscious and extremely fastidious in his personal appearance, a quite clear suggestion of compulsive behaviour.

11
Compatibility

We all have to get along as best we can with those around us, but this is not always as easy as it sounds. In this uncertain world we may sometimes behave in an irrational manner towards someone we have just met for the first time. Somehow, we just do not get along and, at first glance, it can seem as if we may never do so. In effect, this new relationship does not get off to a very good start. As time passes, we find there is something about the association or the other person that prevents it from getting off the ground, no matter how hard we try.

At other times, we find an immediate rapport with our new-found friend. We seem to think alike and can generally have a good time in each other's company.

Sooner or later, at one time or another, men and women all over the world dream of the day that they will meet their soul-mate, fall in love, marry and live happily ever after. Unfortunately, this almost never happens, the dream fades and the idea crumbles. For some it never starts; for a few, it may happen in part or in whole.

It is said that at least once in your life you do meet one 'grand passion', the one love in your life you never, ever forget. You may marry and live happily ever after; such people are the lucky ones, for memories like that do not fade easily.

Those who do not find their soul partner and who have trouble in getting any kind of relationship off the ground may be unable to communicate properly.

But even that should not be too much of a problem because there has to be a certain amount of incompatibility between any two or more people for a variety of reasons.

You may not be able to understand why you have never got along with him, but have always found a rapport with her for example.

Usually, most people simply adjust for this lack of sociability and carry on as best as they can in the circumstances.

However, this sort of an attitude can and does create even more problems, which have a nasty habit of building up without those involved being aware of it. When it does become recognised, it can often be too late to repair the damage.

Compatibility starts in the home environment at an early age.

Here, more than anywhere, all children are taught or learn for themselves the delicate arts of compatibility and negotiation.

Factors to be taken into account include whether the parents are separated or the position of the youngster in the family pecking order.

These early domestic circumstances always have a bearing on the way a child learns to adapt. Their resultant attitude and general behaviour patterns will be carried forward into adult life.

Single children soon acquire good personal confidence as do the oldest ones when brothers or sisters come along. It matters very little whether these children are under a strictly disciplined regimen all the time or are pampered and spoiled.

The second child tends to have slightly less confidence and tends to display slightly more aggression. Usually, this shows when the child has to outshine the older bother or sister or has to prove himself. If allowed, the second child will soon find his niche in life and settle. However, boys tend to be lazier than girls as they develop

A third child has to learn really hard and very quickly indeed.

There is always a great rivalry between brothers and sisters and, the greater the number, the more this will be. Number three child has to work hard to make his mark on the world.

Children's handwriting

Even at a very early age the signs of a positive personality and a growing confident nature beginning to form will be shown in a child's handwriting. With lazy children, or those who feel that almost any effort might go unrewarded, the writing could begin to reflect this with signs of reserve or a lack of confidence.

The writing of intelligent, healthy children who dislike routine is liable to be messy and ill-formed in a seeming contradiction to the writer's ability, perception and facility for learning quickly. This is a reflection of the child's way of protesting against too much restriction and discipline, or he may be registering that he feels he is not receiving enough love and understanding.

A clever child does not always become a clever adult. So when we come to assess the handwriting of a child we must ask questions about the family and immediate environment. The answers we get will show the amount of energy and application that he has put into getting along with those around him. It will also show how much is left for him to cope with his everyday life.

Generally speaking, children are quite adaptable and soon learn to become compatible with their peers. They learn quickly from their mistakes as they adapt and as they progress, their handwriting will also start to reflect this ever-changing series of attitudes. In order to be able to control and compromise with life's challenges, children develop their personal behaviour patterns and character – learning all the time. The speed with which this happens depends on whether the child is basically an introvert or an extrovert.

Introversion is indicated by handwriting that has a leftward or backward slant (unless the child is left-handed). This style is not naturally taught anywhere in the world, so it would have to have been developed by the writer. In any right-handed young child, a left slant to his script always indicates a rebel streak. Once this is noticed, investigate why the child may seem to lack confidence, for this could easily be an unconscious cry for help in one so young. The cause may lie at home or at school. There may be too much discipline from over-demanding parents, brothers and sisters may be treating him badly, he might be bullied by fellow-pupils, or a teacher may be over-exacting.

Handwriting that slants to the right indicates a sociable nature, someone who can get along with just about anyone. This child receives sufficient affection, finds few problems in his scholastic life and holds his own with fellow siblings. He has learned to adapt to his position within the family and deals with problems as they arise in a quiet and confident manner.

Upright handwriting, or a script that varies no more than about five degrees either way from the vertical, shows poise, control and polish. The writer is neither fully outgoing nor wholly withdrawn for he has found his niche and role early in life and is amiable, selective and discriminating. However, he may worry inwardly. He will have some problems in making and maintaining close relationships. There will be very few close and trusted friends, but there will be a wide circle of acquaintances from all walks. This is a personality facet often taken into adult life. Whatever this child's position in the family hierarchy, he tends to accept it as a matter of course.

So, up to a point, our early family and scholastic relationships help define our later emotional attitudes.

But once into adolescence our emotions can run riot at the drop of a hat and mood swings are liable to occur daily or even hourly in some extreme cases, and all of this can be detected in our handwriting.

At some stage in his childhood the average youngster experiments with his handwriting. He tries to emulate his father or mother or that of a teacher he admires the most. He will play with size and style, try various colours of ink or may spend hours developing or just playing with his signature. This junior form of graphomania is normal and, occasionally, may be carried over into adulthood.

During this stage he is likely to adopt a mixed slant. This is a sure sign that the youngster is not sure which way is the right way, which friend is the right friend, or which attitude is the right attitude. It is now that guidance from parents or a teacher will be needed to help channel the child's energies into a positive direction.

As the youngster graduates into his late teens all of these early childhood and adolescent experiences will have helped shape his basic nature. By the time he reaches his early twenties, a more stable personality should be apparent. The character has ripened and matured. Because young people rarely forget the lessons of their childhood and the experience of their teenage years, attitudes and social matters are coloured by an interpretation of those recollections.

This sense of self is a constantly evolving exercise. It is both a conscious and unconscious affair. As a rule, most of us are quite unaware of how we would react in some circumstances until we witness them happening to someone else. We then analyse the reaction of that person from a subjective perspective: would we have done the same thing? When we meet someone for the first time whom we feel are inferior to us we may, consciously or otherwise, act in a superior manner and interpret everything that happens in such a fashion. Similarly, if we are in the company of those whom we consider superior to us the reverse may happen. We quite naturally take on a submissive role. The handwriting of youngsters reflects all of these attitudes and an examination can reveal if this imbalance can be corrected.

Compatibility

When a sample of handwriting is properly analysed it can be very revealing. What one can do with one example of handwriting can obviously be done with another. Therefore, a comparison of two samples will surely show the way the relationship between any two people can be made easier. But compatibility does not stop between two people. It is quite possible to find out whether three, four or even more people are compatible.

Now, this really is very important, it is not just a matter of comparing overall styles with others because while you are very much aware that certain vices and virtues that we associate with specific characteristics are found in a script, you probably have not stopped to think why a writer should express his most personal thoughts in such a manner.

Those who understand the basic principles of compatibility and who try not necessarily to see the viewpoint of another, but try to understand the motives instead and then adjust their attitude and thoughts for this accordingly, are among the most successful people around today – not just in terms of possession, but with an inner harmony.

The higher the compatibility factor between two people, the less hard work is needed for them to co-exist peacefully. The more out of step their writing, the greater the compensatory approach needed. Compromises made at an early stage go far in achieving a good relationship. Both partners must make the effort, for one partner alone cannot carry a relationship.

To enable you to assess compatibility between any two, three or more people these notes should help.

It is also very important to bear in mind the degree of pressure and size of individual handwriting samples because these factors have also be assessed and taken into account.

Righthand slant and righthand slant

Two people who share a forward, right-slanting script will get along quite well. Both are sociable and like to be with people but this combination is also likely to generate a healthy and competitive spirit that can get out of hand sometimes.

Lefthand slant and lefthand slant

When two people who write with a leftward slant come together they must first learn to trust the other and then leave it at that. There is not so much competitiveness between these two for they will tend to allow a lot of latitude. While they can and do make excellent friendships, emotionally, they tend to remain aloof.

Upright style and upright style

Two people who write in the vertical style will get along well for both will understand how the other will react at all times.

There is a place for everything and everything has its place so there will be few fireworks or surprises between these two.

Upright style and righthand slant

When an upright writer enters into a relationship with someone who writes with a forward slant it generally tends to be a very successful liaison. The former will maintain the status quo and keep the other on the straight and narrow most of the time. This should work well for both business and pleasure purposes.

Lefthand slant and righthand slant

When a left-slanting writer tries to get along with the forward-slanting type it will only work if they both allow each other plenty of leeway. The former cannot and does not express his emotions too well but the latter does it all the time. Both of these personalities will have to work at this association to ensure it is a lasting affair.

Lefthand slant and upright style

The left-slanting type should get along fairly well with those who write in the upright style. Both are emotionally reserved but the lead will be shown here by the upright writer. Once the other person realizes this he will come out of his shell for he now knows he can trust his new partner.

Mixed slant

Perhaps we should not leave out those who employ a mixed slant. This writing is consistent with a temporarily unsettled emotional nature who is very much concerned with the mood of the moment. As these folk are basically insecure, relationships of any kind will be a test for them. They are undisciplined and capricious and cannot be trusted to keep cool, calm and collected when needed. Few would accept that in a partner, even another mixed slant type! These are very difficult people with whom you can try to maintain a relationship because they are so unpredictable in their various ways. But, because of their very unpredictability, it might be just the spice needed for a relationship between these people and another who writes in the same style!

12

I-dots, T-bars and Punctuation

Three very special strokes or marks in writing are the i-dots, t-bars and punctuation marks. These are all freehand exercises, in that there is no 'proper' or set manner in which they should be written – only that they should be used. While loops, strokes and ovals and other markings all have their place, these three handwriting features have a very special part to play in analysis because, while you were shown how to make all the other letters, the chances are you were only shown where to place these marks. When you put your pen to paper, you start to write words but may have to stop to either make an i-dot, create a t-bar or place a comma, semi-colon or full stop. Some people finish the word then stop, lift the pen, go back and make the mark, then restart their writing again. Some writers do it as they proceed and join the i-dot or t-bar to the following letter or letters. Yet again, there are those who may omit them altogether.

I-dots
The letter i is written in two parts. First, the stem is written then the dot is placed at the top of that stem. The writer will do this immediately or he will finish the word and then go back to site the dot. A dot must be so made and placed that it fits in with the way the full stop or other punctuation marks are made. It must be noticed, but not so conspicuous that it distracts attention from the text.

The dot over the i first came into use in the thirteenth century. Originally this was to help distinguish it from the letter j. Some historians are of the opinion it might have been the other way, and that the dot was placed over the letter j to ensure errors of identification between it and the letter i could not occur. Probably both letters began to be 'capped' in this way to help readers distinguish between them and the lower-case letters m, n and u which in those days were made as a series of small vertical strokes.

The dot belongs in the upper zone and so it relates to intellect and imagination and, whether placed high or low, with or without pressure, before or after the stem or joined to the next word or words, it will indicate the level of enthusiasm and practicality normally practised by the writer.

It may appear as a dash or look club-like. It can be made like a small wavy mark, as a circle, or can be omitted altogether. Any unusual formation may indicate a writer with special gifts. It is impossible to illustrate the entire range of dots seen in handwriting. However, these descriptions will serve to help the student analyst. In a very short space of time and as experience grows, one is soon able to make accurate surveys. Please remember there could be as many as five or six different types and styles within one sample. This is considered fairly normal.

When a dot is consistently placed to the left of the stem the writer may procrastinate but, when placed to the right of the stem, there is much enthusiasm and impulse in the nature. When placed exactly over the top of the stem, the writing would have to be fairly slow. Therefore, you must expect to find much attention to detail and a precise attitude.

A high-flying dot always signifies idealism, imagination and strong creativity. If it is made like a small wavy line, there will be an ever-present sense of humour in the writer's character.

Club-like or dash-style marks tell of rather earthy passions. The writer has a temper and is often irritable. The heavier these are made, the more this will be so.

While it does happen, it is rare to see lightly made marks like this unless the rest of the letter is also written very lightly. I-dots that are lightly made suggest a sensitive mature which is not assertive enough when necessary.

Arc-like dots suggest sensitivity. When the arc is to the right, the writer is perceptive and often intuitive. When the arc is to the left he is sensitive to criticism, introspective and wary of new people in his circle. If there is a hint of angularity in the arc there may be an acid tongue and sarcasm.

A dot joined to the following letter is the sure mark of a swift and perceptive mind. This is someone who, once a project starts, has to finish it and does not brook much opposition. This mark is also a sign of intelligence.

The circle dot belongs to the food fad, the artistic, the young or the emotional misfit, someone who has to be the centre of attention at all times. The writer may have some manual ability or dexterity. The older the writer the more he may be slightly eccentric. In essence, the circle i-dot implies narcissism.

When the stem of the letter i is made consistently smaller than the rest of the middle zone writing, the writer worries a lot, has feelings of inadequacy and lacks confidence.

If the lower case i is used as the personal pronoun instead of the usual capital letter, the writer is immature, lacks drive and enthusiasm and undervalues what few natural talents he does have. He is also easily led.

T-bars

Some graphologists are of the opinion that the letter t is the most important letter of the alphabet and this is supported by several published books and a wide-ranging series of privately prepared papers devoted entirely to it.

The letter has had a fascinating history, and was once the origin of the letter x, often used as a personal mark of recognition – the signature of the masses or the illiterate. Like the letter i the letter t also has a free stroke – the bar. In ancient times the letter t was first written like a lower case letter c. To avoid confusion the stem was straightened and the bar was added.

From the way this letter is constructed and how the bar is added, we may detect ambition, control, discipline, drive, enthusiasm, intelligence, speed, enthusiasm and willpower.

The letter t, like the letter i, is created in two parts. First the stem is made then the bar should be placed across the stem. Most writers will do this immediately, or will finish the word and then go back to place the bar. The bar should be written and placed so that, like the i-dot, it fits in with the way the full stop or other punctuation marks are made.

The t-bar also has to be written so that it is noticed, but not too conspicuously in case it distracts attention from the rest of the text. It is obvious when it is omitted altogether.

There are more than fifty ways of writing the stem of the letter t and, with the wide variety of cross-bars that can be added to it, the possibilities are significantly increased. Once again, it is not possible to illustrate them all. Those referred to here are the principal variations. The reader will be able to trace the type, but is then invited to make his own decision in terms of variations on any of the themes he may encounter.

The short bar is indicative of poor drive and enthusiasm and there will be some reserve or caution in the writer's nature. The long cross-bar shows confidence and control. The writer is ambitious and usually has plenty of energy to carry out his plans.

Heavy cross-bars always refer to a determined nature. As a rule, there is often a selfish streak and the writer is inclined to be rather a domineering type.

A lightly made cross-bar shows the writer to be easily led and influenced and quite likely to have a shy or retiring nature.

A wavy cross-bar shows a lighter nature, a sense of humour and a personality who enjoys a bit of fun. However, when the bar seems to be knotted in any way, the writer will possess a critical and persistent approach. The person is tenacious and, once he starts a project he will finish it.

A cross-bar that is made from the base of the stem in a forward and upward curve to the right indicates someone who may not always be as truthful as they should – especially in times of stress. The bar made from the base of the stem in an upward but backward curve to the left shows an element of self-blame, introspection or unnecessary worry.

A low-set t-bar implies few active ambitions, a lack of push and energy to achieve. Set in the middle of the stem, the writer has medium capability but needs to be encouraged to actively pursue his interests. The high-set bar indicates ambition, leadership and imagination.

A concave t-bar is often encountered with those who have either strong or repressed emotions and physical passions. The depth of pressure must be assessed before making a pronouncement. Convex t-bars reveal poor self-control, often someone with a built-in lazy streak or emotional instability. This writer can be rather wilful at times.

An ascending stroke from left to right, like an upward pointing arrow, shows optimism, passion and enthusiasm. Descending bars always shows a stubborn, persistent, aggressive and pessimistic nature. If the stroke is light, this is eased considerably but, if it is a heavy stroke, this is emphasized.

When a cross-bar is made high above the stem the implication is someone with unrealistic ideas. This writer allows imagination to rule in his plans much more than is good for him. With heavy pressure there will be a strong sense of adventure; this writer is fond of physical activities.

Should t-bars be omitted altogether, the writer may be absent-minded, careless or even rebellious. It is quite normal for a few t-bars to be missing in any sample of handwriting.

The stem of the letter t may be created in a number of different ways. These variations, coupled with the selection of cross-bar interpretations, go a long way to prove the importance of this letter.

A loop at the top of the stem shows sensitivity to any kind of criticism, a person who needs continuous encouragement largely because of too much self-doubt. Where you find a looped stem and no cross-bar it shows strong emotions, often to the detriment of common sense or reason.

A tent-like t-stem implies a stubborn nature and a closed mind. This writer does not give way easily, even if he knows he is in the wrong. He may like the attention this attitude brings.

The letter t may appear in a variety of star-shapes or knots, and when made in any of these styles it implies a tough, thorough and persistent type who prefers his own way of going about things. If the cross-bar is absent, this will be less so, but if the bar is present there also be some obstinacy.

The stem of the letter t made like a narrow inverted letter u is a sign of a slow, deliberate type who moves and works entirely to his own satisfaction. Nothing shifts him, he has one speed – his own. He is also reluctant to implement or accept changes.

It is always worth spending time investigating all the variations of the letters i and t in a sample of handwriting. But do bear in mind that these are all single factors among many others.

The slant and pressure of the script, together with the general presentation, all have to taken into account as well. Remember the golden rule of analysis. No single feature of handwriting, however strong it may appear, should ever be taken in isolation.

Punctuation

Most punctuation marks have to follow on at the end of a word or sentence to divide that sentence, emphasize a point, or end part of the message.

A sudden freedom of expression is allowed to the writer at this point, and it is a most revealing and significant element in graphological analysis. Punctuation, or the lack of it, is a sign of attention to detail. Most intelligent, educated writers take care as their writing progresses. If they become too concerned with their message then details like commas or full stops take on a secondary value, but there is no corresponding reduction in their intelligence.

When writers meticulously dot every i and cross every t they are showing that they conform, and do what is expected of them in much the same way as when they were still in school. The lessons learned then have stuck with them through into adulthood.

The correct position for a punctuation mark is in line with the base of the preceding letter, and when placed like this it shows a balanced outlook at the time of writing. However, when this small feature suddenly flies high up above the base-line then the writer's mood was obviously quite cheerful and carefree. The full stop or comma placed well below the base-line implies depression, perhaps pessimism, and quite often, a tired writer. The rest of the handwriting should provide enough information for you to assess this.

Handwriting that does not vary a lot suggests good control, but when punctuation differs at the end of a letter, in comparison to the start, it indicates a mood change. So a letter with neat and tidy punctuation at the start but that is all over the place by the end suggests that the writer's initial control has faded.

Excessive punctuation means that the writer likes to show-off, someone who exaggerates, and could be over-emphatic in his speech as well. It is the mark of a worrier, someone who cannot or will not give up, even long after a matter has been resolved.

Punctuation marks omitted or put in the wrong place in low-level handwriting shows poor thinking, or someone who cannot be bothered with details. There may be a rebel streak or the writer is just plain awkward, enjoys being 'different' and likes to take the opposing view for the sake of it.

To ensure the punctuation that is present is correct, you have to read *what* is written *as* it is written and *not* what you think the writer meant at the time. The best way to achieve this is to read what is written aloud to yourself very carefully. This always brings out the errors.

Good or poor punctuation can mean different things in different styles. Good punctuation in a neat and tidy handwriting has much less value than poor punctuation in heavy-pressure writing.

A full stop placed after a signature, whether the full name has been used or just the forename, always speaks of the writer who must have the last word.

13
Doodles

It is said that one picture paints a thousand words, and nowhere is this more graphically illustrated than when we come to analyse doodles. In recent times, those engaged in graphological research have paid a lot more attention to this novel but often neglected area, and much has been discovered.

A doodle is a graphical expression of an unconscious association. It helps relieve tension, stress and anxiety. As a result, we may obtain relief from pain, pleasure or sadness as we doodle. Whether the cause is emotional, psychological, sexual or social, we often doodle while waiting for something to happen. More often than not most of us tend to make these little scribbles while we are on the telephone. We draw them anywhere and everywhere: blotting paper, scratch pads, lists, magazine borders or anything else to hand when the urge to doodle overcomes us. Some psychologists maintain that the doodle is a physical projection of our inner or hidden emotional desires. Because of this, your doodles may be taken into account if or when your company asks you to take part in personality and character assessments.

Doodles are not handwriting, but little scribbles or drawings. Generally speaking, they are simply collections of blobs, dots, lines and squiggles, but made in a repetitive action. Most people have what may seem to be a favourite doodle which they draw over and over again. As we shall show, the doodle is quite possibly a reflection of our inner, emotional worries and fears which, in some cases, are not always properly resolved.

A repeated design, no matter what the overall pattern, is simply the writer's way of helping to ease the current tension or take his mind off the problem and has nothing to do with its source. Most people feel a strong need to do something as they think a matter through. Thus the doodle is a graphical manifestation associated with a tangible or intangible problem, an expression of the unconscious state while conscious attention is elsewhere.

There are some people who do not doodle, but they are very few. These people are usually controlled, direct, precise and straight to the point in their manner at all times.

A graphologist will look first at the position of the drawing and note precisely where it is before he looks at what it is.

Doodles made on the left-hand side of the paper suggests a writer who exhibits some slight inner reserve. He has a cautious approach where people are concerned and may not make new friends readily. The past means a lot to this writer; he might have trouble trying to forget incidents or people from the past. He is not cold and neither is he unresponsive. He simply cannot display affection in public places and, even when alone with his favourite person, he has some difficulty in this area.

When the doodle is placed more to the right-hand side of the page the writer is more outgoing, and socially motivated. The future holds more for this person, he always looks forward, always ready for tomorrow. He is a progressive who likes and needs to be with others. The past holds very little for this writer.

A doodle in the centre of the paper shows an extroverted nature. This type must be noticed and will ensure he is if others forget he is there.

If the doodle is more to the top of the page the writer is quite an enthusiast and little gets him down. He does not always have his feet on the floor, for he is full of new ideas all the time. When the doodle is placed more to the bottom of a page the writer is less outgoing and, even if he has talent, does not always push himself or his ideas forward.

Drawings made with obvious heavy pressure show the writer very much responsive to the prevailing mood of the moment. He may, of course, be under more stress than he might admit and there will be some controlled aggression or a display of temper if rubbed the wrong way. He will also be rather serious – certainly at the time of creating his design.

Medium pressure is the average and suggests a fairly balanced and reasonable inner nature. The subject matter of the doodle might be a guide to any discrepancies in the writer's normal behaviour patterns. A light pressure indicates a receptive and sensitive personality, perhaps not always able to absorb experiences and someone who can be easily influenced.

Erratic pressure is a sign of instability, someone on a high one minute and on a low the next. While this pressure remains erratic the writer remains unreliable.

When a particular design is repeated time and time again all over the paper the writer is emotionally or mentally compulsive. This is not the time for him to make cold, hard decisions, certainly where people are concerned. The mood of the moment rules all.

A common factor seen frequently is a drawing that has been shaded in part or in whole. This suggests anxiety, inner worry or a fear of some kind nagging at the writer, founded or unfounded. He will have probably convinced himself of all the negative views of whatever is worrying him and cannot see a way out. This is also the case when, instead of shading, a writer underlines everything. Here, the line is used as a prop on which he can stand to prevent himself sinking further. This is a sense of protection. If the line is on the top of the sketch, it should be read as a sign of protection from the wrath of those above.

Sometimes a doodle incorporates a number of different designs. This suggests a vivid imagination with interest in many different areas. The writer has sufficiently diverse talents to warrant his many faceted patterns. The dominant pattern will emphasize either the problem(s) or a personality trait – or both.

Colours

Doodles can be drawn almost anywhere at any time and, in general, they are drawn in the same colour as the writer's normal pen. However, some doodlers like to use different colours when they make their creations.

We have discussed the use of colour in the normal writing mode elsewhere, but when doodling certain colours take on accentuated meanings, and this is especially so where it is obvious that the writer has deliberately chosen a colour – or series of colours – to execute his drawing. In each case colours mean more if they are chosen as the first or primary colour of the doodle.

To deliberately choose or use red means energy and sexuality and it acts as a stimulative. Pink shows a more feminine side of nature in both men and women. Blue is an indication of the more reflective influence, while green implies resentment or envy at the time the doodle was created.

Yellow is often used when money or material matters are involved. The inference is that yellow is the same colour as gold. In an entirely different area one may find yellow is used when health problems are the root cause of the worry. (This has been noted in a hospital environment.) Brown is always used to define a need for security and plain old-fashioned common sense.

Violet or mauve is an indication that the doodler needs, or must have, more emotional consistency in his life. These shades are also a sign of great inner sensitivity. If drawn by a woman she will have that extra femininity; if used by a man, he is likely to have a very gentle nature, naturally creative or artistic.

Grey is a neutral or impartial symbol. As a rule this colour can reflect depression, or a (temporarily) defeated mode.

When black is used the writer is anxious and tense. When he does finally decide on a course of action to restore the status quo it may be an all or nothing attempt.

It must be stressed that a complete character assessment is not possible from one, two or even more doodles. One should be able to discern a number of qualities and traits but these should be regarded only as pointers – these guidelines are not meant as tablets of stone. With this in mind here are some aids to help you assess doodles.

Aeroplanes Aeroplanes are basically phallic symbols. An airliner suggests the writer just wants to get away from it all. There may be a holiday looming or it may have just finished. A war plane is an indication of violence. A helicopter might imply indecision.

Animals Animals imply a fondness for them in general terms. The doodler may want one for a pet or the nature associated with the animal might refer to the problem or his personality. Thus, an elephant may mean a weight problem; a lion, leadership; a monkey, a sense of humour; a parrot, a sense of humour.

Arrows Arrows or ascending straight lines show ambition and aspirations. Arrows used as part of a design imply an element of calculation in the doodler. When the arrows or lines point downward, the negative side of things is presently occupying the mind. A small series of lines together suggest a blunt, no-nonsense type.

Birds Birds represent a desire to fly away and leave it all behind. Big birds, or birds of prey imply feelings of resentment. This writer can wait a long time to get even.

Boats Boats suggest a similar disposition as birds. However, a large liner shows a love of luxury. Speedboats suggest an adventurous nature – sail-boats mean a dreamer. The writer might be inwardly lonely.

Books Books that are drawn open show a healthy interest for furthering one's knowledge. Closed books still show a desire to know more but this doodler writer can also keep a secret. A series of books implies method and order and, possibly, a bit of a show-off.

Boxes Boxes indicate a controlled and controlling nature. The writer is rather precise, logical and practical. When any of the boxes have been shaded in, not unlike a chess board, there will be an added attention to detail. Shading admits a more emotional approach.

Body parts When body parts are continually drawn it shows an interest in that part of the body at the time. In older people it may be a health matter. In the young it may be sexual: adolescent boys may draw breasts while young girls draw the penis or a phallic symbol.

Circles All completed circles are a symbol of independence; uncompleted circles suggest a more flexible approach; the doodler may well cooperate, but only up to a point. Drawing circles is also a sign of a lazy streak. The author of any circular doodle tends to be a dreamer. Rows and rows of circles show a desire to solve problems without too much hassle. Circles can also refer to a sexual problem. There is very little aggression here.

Clouds Small, unshaded fluffy clouds denote escapism. If filled in, the writer has difficulty when dealing with his emotional and sexual problems. A whole series of clouds of any shape or size indicates a well-disposed personality. If rain is shown falling from them, the author can spend a lot of time trying to cross bridges before he gets to them.

Dots Drawings made with lots of dots show the ability to concentrate. If linked by lines, the writer may be frustrated, unable to bring a project or other aim to fruition. The picture may be symbolic here.

Eyes How the eye is drawn is significant because it may mean anything from selfishness and self-absorption to sexual problems. Female eyes with long lashes suggest a flirtatious nature and, if heavy eyebrows are also drawn, there is a sexual connotation. Eyes are the mirror of the soul. Once again, the drawing might give some additional clues.

Faces When a face is drawn in profile it can mean a recent or current relationship difficulty. Happy faces mean all is well but sad or serious faces imply a lack of cooperation with or by others is at the root. This doodler dislikes being subjected to the caprices of others. When a hat covers the head, or one eye, the author is showing a self-protective streak. Self-portraiture is always an extension of the ego whether or not it is complementary.

Fences Fences are meant to keep things in. Whenever a fence appears, whatever it surrounds is the probable cause of the worry. If it is a name, then the person with that name is not being very helpful.

Figures Doodling with numbers suggests money problems unless the same figure is constantly repeated within the pattern. In this case the same number repeatedly doodled could indicate the amount of people or things in the way of settling problems to hand.

The figure one is often written as a substitute for the personal pronoun I. The I represents our ego – too many number 1s in a doodle implies a certain amount of egocentricity.

Fish Fish usually mean a realistic attitude. The writer will take on any reasonable challenge to his abilities. If there are many fish in the picture the author is inclined to be a busybody.

Flowers All flower drawings have an emotionally orientated preoccupation associated with them. The flower itself may denote how much this so. It would help to have some knowledge of the language of the flowers sometimes. This doodler is often a sentimentalist. Heavy pressure may have some sexual meaning. Light pressure shows a desire for a return to what a relationship used to mean.

Frames Frames or borders placed around a doodle acts like a fence but here, the writer is torn between a desire for more freedom but with an inner wish for more basic protection and security. A fence can have holes, but frames and borders do not.

Hearts Hearts are always a sign of emotional vulnerability very near the surface and often appear in a doodler's repertoire shortly after a relationship has broken up. The more heart shapes there are, the more emotional the writer. If hearts are drawn one inside the other, it is a sign of a need for more affection to be given or received.

Houses House doodles symbolize safety and security. The more detailed the drawing the more the doodler is an idealist. If a garden is included, then a very short path to the door indicates a more settled nature while a long path shows a guarded one.

Ladders Ladders suggest a social climber. The position of anything, or any person drawn on one of the rungs could represent the doodler, how far he has come, or has yet to go.

Lucky charms A doodle that illustrates any symbol of luck, like a four-leaf clover, a horse shoe or the number 7, suggests the writer feels cheated. In some ways, it is a cry for help for the doodler feels it is about time his luck changed for the better. Extra effort by him is not included in this desire for improvement.

Mazes Doodles involving a maze or a web-like pattern suggests inner conflict. There may be frustration at a lack of achievement and the author may be confused as to his next step in such matters.

Money Most of the time a doodle involving money is a sure sign that the doodler wants more of it. Money usually means comfort, ease and security. Doodles of money, their symbols ($ £) signs or coins imply a degree of personal greed or selfishness in other ways; the writer may be unsympathetic to the wants and needs of others.

Music Musical notes are rarely made by those who have little interest in music. The suggestion is that the writer has creative talents directed toward the arts. An excess of symbols could also mean a sense of humour.

Names Doodling your own name suggests a strong ego because you think a lot about yourself. If one of the names is encircled there may be some extra worry concerning someone you know with that name. Youngsters often enjoy doodling with their name or signature. It is always worth comparing the signature with the doodled version.

Patterns Symmetrical patterns suggest the organiser – the more complex the doodle, the better the executive power. When shading of any kind is included the writer's sex drive may be currently lacking.

Snakes are a sign of wisdom and sexual prowess. If coiled snakes are drawn, it shows a certain amount of rebellion and a stubborn attitude. A snake at rest, long and flexible, shows the writer is more open to suggestion.

Spirals Spirals are usually created from small or large circular formats. When expanded from the smaller version the writer would have been full of tension, as if expecting the unexpected but ready to meet the challenge. This is symbolic of expansion and optimism. If the spirals are inter-twined or gradually become smaller things may be too much for the doodler and suggests depression or a negative outlook.

Squares As a rule, squares indicate aggression and constructive ability. Whether interlocked, side by side or one on top of another this writer does not take kindly to opposition and likes an ordered life. Squares drawn within squares are suggestive of frustration. The doodler is unable to resolve current difficulties.

Stars Stars are frequent subjects for doodlers. They imply an ambitious nature, one who will succeed and who may well bend a few rules to make sure they achieve their aim. This is the sign of a very determined and aggressive person but it may be all in the mind. If possible, note the colour or writing style for further clues.

Steps Steps are a sign of sexual problems and an ambitious nature. If the steps rise to a dead end it means that the doodler's plans may not succeed and that they may have to be re-worked.

If a series of steps are drawn side by side and fill a page from side to side the author is a fairly flexible type, someone who is not put off by failure and is always ready to try again.

Trees An American lecturer in psychology devised a special test many years ago involving trees. He discovered over 25 ways to sketch or doodle a tree. In his analyses he reached a very high degree of accuracy in his findings.

The type of tree drawn represents the inner nature. If leaves or branches point upward, it implies an optimistic type. When drawn pointing down, the writer may be depressed. A well-rounded tree shows a pleasant sociable nature; pointed or hard-angled versions suggests a touchy personality. If ground is drawn around the base it can mean anxiety, reserve or unrealistic thinking.

Triangles Triangles imply aggression, ambition and energy. For many, it is also a sexual symbol. This doodler has a constructive mind, with a good level of perception. He knows how to deal with people and loves solving problems. He is also quite prepared to sacrifice anything or anyone to achieve his personal aims.

Waves If the waves are predominantly garland the drawing suggests an open and friendly nature. Arcade waves are an indication of a secretive nature, someone who knows how to cover his tracks. If anything is shown in the water, things or people, it or they can represent the source of the problem.

If these items are drawn under the water, the doodler cannot yet see any real answer to the worry at the time the doodle is made.

Wheels When wheels are properly drawn so they are different to a circle the doodle shows mental alertness. If the wheels are depicted as rolling forward it indicates independence. Wheels shown rolling backwards suggest the writer to be overly concerned with his past glories.

Words When the same words are constantly repeated they often show the cause of the problem, especially if a name is discernible. Try to use basic graphology techniques or compare the doodled words with a written version.

14
The Signature

It is fitting that the last chapter should be an analysis of the signature, its history and its meaning. When you think about it, it is the last thing anyone writes once they have finished their message. It is that final moment, the last word or words, that special moment as the actor finally leaves the stage. And how it shows. The signature indicates how the writer would like to be seen by the outside world and is a reflection of the 'outer' image that he tries to project.

The main text of the letter, message, missive or whatever, is a reflection of the writer's emotional, mental and physical state and is a good indication of the real or 'inner' man.

You must always exercise a great deal of caution when asked to assess a single signature, especially in the absence of any other example from the same writer. Often, there are significant differences in the way the main text of a letter is written and the way it is signed. It is also worth remembering that many people use two different signatures. Many businessmen have devised one for their professional life (and image) while retaining another for their more private and personal affairs.

At a very early age we try to adopt a specific style of handwriting. We soon learn to modify the basic alphabet here, add little bits and pieces there until eventually, we establish a style we like. It becomes as much a part of us as the way we smile, shake hands or walk. This is especially true of the signature for, in our early days we probably practised writing our name more often than anything else. We practised on almost any old scrap of paper we could get our hands on, not necessarily to learn to write better, but for the sheer pleasure of seeing our name on paper. We will have tried to copy different styles used by adults in our immediate circle, parents, brothers or sisters, aunts or uncles, even teachers. This early form of junior graphomania is something almost all people carry over into adult life.

Today, in most civilized countries, the law and society recognize our signature as being unique. When someone tries to forge another person's name it can earn the most severe penalties. By this action society acknowledges that a signature does, in fact, reflect a writer's personality and character. Incidentally, a signature is one of the most difficult parts of our personal writing style to forge, and it is usually where the fraud investigator will start his examination.

Looking back over the centuries it is now fairly obvious that, after the evolution of speech and then formal language, writing would have developed as a matter of course anyway. It had to. In turn, printing systems developed and now, all those years later, computers now rule the roost in terms of modern communication.

Back in those early days when trade started to become commonplace and the first commercial contacts with others began, markings of some kind were needed to define ownership of goods, both before and after a sale. Labels of clay, either in colour or bearing a symbol began to be used.

These labels soon began to have seals attached to them and it did not take that long for the seal to become recognised as a symbol of identity and ownership. Before much longer it also became the mark of the personality of the trader. Soon, these traders became known through their personal seal for their fairness, honesty or otherwise.

Today, this seal has been translated into the modern corporate logo. The most famous of all logos throughout the world is now known to be the "M" arch of McDonalds Restaurants.

In the non-commercial area your own flag is instantly recognised by fellow nationals. Perhaps the Red Cross, and the interlinked rings of the Olympic logo are also quickly appreciated.

The latest innovation in the history of the seal is taking place even now. Daily, almost everywhere computers are being connected to the world-wide Internet. To talk and receive messages you have to be recognised by the latest and most modern signature of them all – the computerised E-mail address.

And a study of how people achieve their identity on this enormous web of communication has started already.

However, while the seal in itself should not be regarded as the beginning of handwriting as such, it is easy to see how it has its place as one of the many ancestors of modern writing. With the original idea of these seals in mind, it is easy to see how, over the years, handwriting has become so inextricably linked with character and personality.

Your signature says much to the graphologist in the same way but, because it is also your personal name as well, it yields far more information because your signature stands for you, the writer.

It is your persona on paper.

Whenever possible, always try to have more than one signature to work on. One written when the writer is in good health, or trouble-free, can be quite different to one written when the writer is depressed or out of sorts. For example, unless you know otherwise the signature of a newly married woman can be mis-interpreted. She may not have decided on a new format to represent her real feelings yet: she may not like or have become used to her new surname. She finds it hard to adjust and, like many others in her position, she is likely to pen her first name larger than her new surname.

While the signature generally tends to remain basically the same, once the author has decided on its design, it can and does vary if the writer is disturbed in any way through an emotional upset or a bout of ill-health.

People in public service or those whose career requires them to have to constantly sign documentation often have two signatures. The one they use at work reflects their business status and image. Their other, or normal signature will reveal their private and personal attitude to life.

The signature is the most frequent example of handwriting and unique to us as an individual. No two signatures are exactly identical, any more than there are two sets of identical finger prints. For a proper analysis, a few lines of the writer's usual writing should be compared with the signature. It is better to have several examples written at different times because handwriting does vary so much.

Position
Where a signature is placed in relation to what has been written has a great significance.

If the signature is placed slightly to the right of centre and at a reasonable distance from the last line the writer will enjoy a relatively outgoing life, show initiative and sociability.

When placed exactly in the centre of the page he will like to be in the front of everything as much as possible. But, underneath it all he will display an element of caution or bluff that only those close to him will notice.

When a writer puts his signature at the extreme right-hand side of the paper it shows a lively and active personality. However, there might be some impatience with the 'system' because he does not take too kindly to petty bureaucracy.

A signature placed to the left of centre indicates caution and a slightly self-defensive or self-protective side to the writer's nature. This defensiveness really shows itself if the writer is challenged for some reason – guilty or not.

A signature placed to the extreme left of the paper suggests a lack of confidence, reserve or a slightly withdrawn nature. However, this position may be in keeping with the company policy where the writer is employed. Make enquiries about this because, if it is the case, then this writer does not show much initiative to free himself of the work-place influence when away from it.

When the signature is written very close to the last line of the letter, the writer believes in and is being honest about what he has just written. This is especially so when the letter is of a personal nature. The further away the signature is from the last line of text the less the writer wants to be associated with what he has said – and what he has said may not be wholly truthful either.

When the size of the signature is smaller than the text it suggests introversion. The writer is sensitive and mild but he may also be a schemer who sets out to deliberately give such an impression to gain an advantage.

When the signature is larger than the main body of text it shows a confident, determined and forceful character who moves smoothly along in life: little fazes him.

If the signature is quite considerably larger than the text, then the writer will exhibit selfishness and have an overbearing outlook. People like this are not always nice to know, they always seem to be over-confident, proud or even pretentious.

A clear, easily understood and well balanced signature (see fig. 1 overleaf) without any embellishment indicates a reliable but fairly conservative nature.

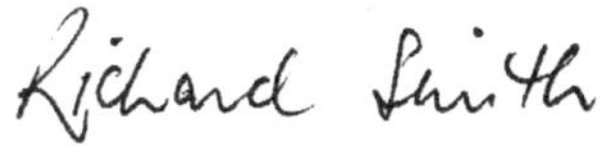

Richard Smith

fig 1

An over-emphasized or exaggerated signature (fig. 2) indicates a healthy ego but often hides an inner inferiority complex. In such a case it would help to look at the rest of the handwriting for further evidence to support this.

fig 2

People who have an illegible signature, one that cannot be read or understood (fig. 3), clearly show bad manners, rudeness and downright selfishness. This writer has very little regard for his reader. He cares only for what he has written and not for you.

fig 3

When the signature is written with the initials and the surname (fig. 4) it suggests a rather formal nature. This writer is a careful and rather conservative sort who prefers to stick with the rule book and is largely self-protective.

fig 4

The writer who signs all of his forenames and surname in full (fig. 5 overleaf) tends to be a snob, pompous and full of his own importance. The world must revolve about him at all times. He is very full of himself.

fig 5

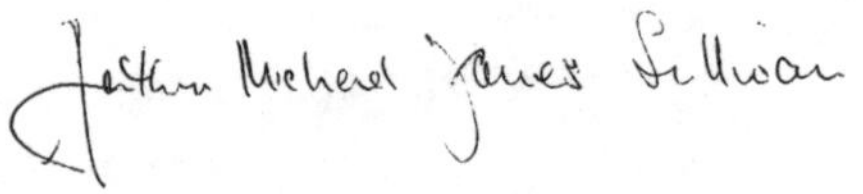

Jostkin Micheal Jones Sullivan

When there is a full stop at the end of the signature it is the writer's (unconscious) way of telling you that this is the last word in the matter and that it is now a closed affair.

If a colon or semi-colon is used instead of the full stop, the writer is probably prepared to continue with the dialogue, but is reluctant to pursue the matter any further at present.

Underlining

Originally, the underline or flourish after a signature was first introduced as a defence against forgery. Those who underline their signature are often cautious people who tend to use it as a kind of prop to help support their ideas in much the same way as the lead-in stroke (see page 68).

Many analysts feel that underlining the signature implies a sense of confidence. In some cases this may be so, but that confidence is often born of doubt, however slight or strong the message may seem. Otherwise why does the writer use it? A heavy line (see fig. 6) implies a sense of energy and enthusiasm but much depends on the position and style of the line. But this is often a sense of limitation, for this writer does not permit too much intimacy until he is completely sure of you. This is especially so in business communications. This writer may not allow or use first names in (business) conversation.

Lindsay Sibbald

fig 6

When the underlining is extended to encircle the signature (fig. 7) then it should be read as a symbol of anxiety and withdrawal. This is a symbol of a lonely and self-imposed isolated nature and there may well be difficulty in mixing socially.

A line over the signature, an overscore (fig. 8), is not seen very often. This shows a writer with a strong need for self-protection. He

fig 7

fig 8

can be selfish and may be wary of change. If there is an underscore and an overscore (see fig. 9), it is difficult for the writer to trust other people – even those who think they are close to him. He is usually lonely, reserved and suspicious of the motives of those around him.

A double line of emphasis under a signature (fig. 10) shows determination and a strong desire to win recognition and status that the writer feels he deserves. He may be talented but it does not follow that he always uses such gifts wisely. This is yet another indication of selfishness.

fig 9

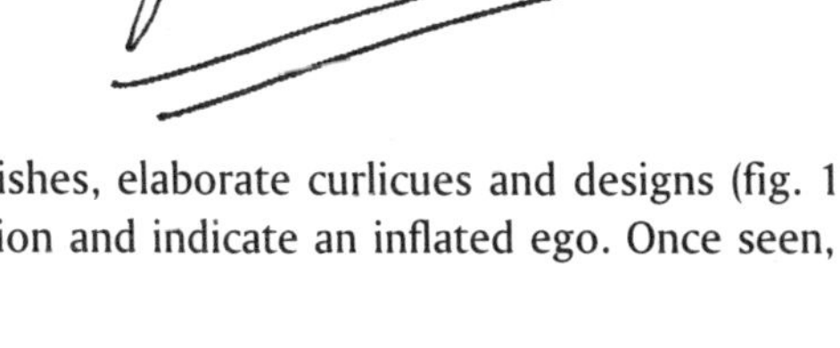

fig 10

All flourishes, elaborate curlicues and designs (fig. 11 overleaf) are ostentation and indicate an inflated ego. Once seen, this signature is not easily forgotten. It shows the writer has poor taste, is a snob and overly pretentious.

fig 11

A short line placed under the first name only suggests the writer enjoys informality. When placed under the surname only the writer prefers to keep things formal until he decides otherwise.

When a forename has more than one syllable and there is a short line under the last part of the name the writer does not like it to be abbreviated (Peter, not Pete; Victoria, not Vicky). When a line is written through a name or a part of the name, the writer has problems getting along with others. Initially, he may seem deceptive or rather shallow. In a woman's writing scoring through the family name suggests the partnership is not currently a happy one.

Signature Slant

The right-hand or forward slant in handwriting suggests a social and naturally gregarious nature. So when the text slants mainly to the right but the signature slants backwards to the left, there will be some difference between the writer's natural personality and the way he appears to others. Here, the writer tries to curb his natural spontaneity and suppress emotional responses. There will be an unnatural air of reserve.

The reverse of this, a left-slanted script with a right-slanted signature means the writer is basically outwardly affectionate but only on the surface. What you see is not what you get because this writer is playing a part. He is inwardly cold and reserved and may even seem quite demonstrative or easy-going but it is all a cultivated front.

When you see upright handwriting accompanied by a left-slanted signature it suggests the actor who really does know how to hide his true, inner feelings. He will always appear poised, charming and confident the majority of the time – but even this is a very carefully controlled act.

Vertical handwriting with a right slanting signature suggests a slightly less controlled nature, but the writer is still a little wary when it comes to dealing with those around him. He will be a trifle more demonstrative when he so chooses. This style is often employed by those people who prefer to work on their own or in the background.

Signatures that rise upward show optimism, especially when also firmly underlined. Descending signatures imply the writer is in poor spirits; tired and depressed at the time of writing.

When any of the lower zone strokes in a signature extend to the right it implies an outgoing, friendly and good natured sort.

When the upper zone strokes and loops of a signature reach high and to the left it suggests the writer has plenty of high ideals and aspirations, but unless the rest of the text confirms it, not enough follow-through to realize these dreams.

When the upper zone extenders stretch high and to the right the writer will be actively ambitious much of the time. Handwriting with heavy pressure will accentuate this while a light pressure eases this inner tension somewhat.

Signatures written with a mixed slant shows an unstable person. This writer is unreliable, subject to the mood of the moment and inwardly unsettled.

Capital Letters

When the capital letters of the name are over-emphasized expect materialism and poor taste. The writer craves status and position and is prepared to do almost anything to attain it.

Capital letters that are slightly above average size suggest the writer is self-obsessed. He does his best to cultivate people he feels he can use in his drive for success.

When capital letters are the same size as the rest of the name the writer is inclined to be rather modest, hardworking but not very ambitious.

Small capitals indicate someone who tends to undervalue himself. This writer tends to drift from one day to the next and quietly gets on with it.

When you see a signature, or any other part of the letter, that has what seems to be an X formation or a series of Xs within it, like an unfinished loop, the writer could be weighed down with problems that affect his emotional well-being. He may have been recently bereaved, a long-time relationship may have broken up, or a business association has come to nothing. The X formation frequently indicates a quite serious loss of personal esteem and a very low emotional state. In most cases this writer needs expert counselling. Frame your advice very carefully indeed for this sign is often found in the notes left behind by those who have committed suicide.

Conclusion

Now that you have read the book please do not put it on the shelf and forget all about it until the next time you want to use it.

You must practise, and practise regularly if you are to achieve any kind of proficiency. Every day, almost everywhere, you will have an opportunity to study handwriting or people as they write a letter, a short note or just put their signature to a form. On the bus or train, watch how people hold their pens. And if they doodle, so much the better – try to get a good look at it. Also try to remember what has been said about the colour of ink and paper – it all helps to sharpen your perception. Note the sort of writing instrument people seem to prefer. Many young people, school children and the more mature students alike study their notes/homework/essays on their way to and from their place of education. And then there are the crossword fanatics...

Look at bus or train conductors (if there are any left where you are) or drivers and inspectors and note what they prefer or may be made to use. When making purchases in a shop, note what the cashier uses or offers for you to sign a bank card purchase form. To spend time in these observations makes a journey go a little faster or the day with a swing. But it all offers a wealth of information about people as they go on their daily round. However, this exercise is a trifle one-sided because you may not always be able to ask questions of those who do catch your eye because of something special associated with them.

Pluck up courage, be brave, ask your question and tell them why. You might not only make a new friend and verify a graphological trait, you will also satisfy your curiosity in this fascinating new study. Remember, each character trait in a sample of handwriting is only a clue. It should never be taken in isolation as representing a feature of personality. An occasional sign may mean just that. Further, do remember that all aspects of personality have positive and negative facets. The whole sample must be evaluated thoroughly and very carefully.

Bear in mind that what you have before you reflects the mood and disposition of the writer at the time of writing. Do not jump to conclusions. But do have fun.

Suggested Further Reading

Hill, B., *Graphology* (Robert Hale, London, 1981).

Jacoby, H. J., *Self-Knowledge through Handwriting* (Dent, London, 1941).

Marne, P., *Crime and Sex in Handwriting* (Constable, London, 1981).

Mendel, A. O., *Personality in Handwriting* (Stephen Daye Press, New York, 1982).

McNichol, A. and Nelson, J. A., *Handwriting Analysis, Putting It to Work for You*, (Contemporary Books, Inc, Chicago, 1991).

Olyanova, N., *Handwriting Tells* (Peter Owen, London, 1970).

Roman, K., *Handwriting, A Key to Personality* (Pantheon, New York, 1952).

Singer, E., *A Manual of Graphology* (Duckworth, London 1969).

West, P., *Graphology, Understanding What Handwriting Reveals* (Aquarian Press, London, 1981).

West, P., *You and Your Handwriting*, (Allison & Busby, London, 1986).

Index